"Billy Joe!" shouted Bitsy, as she climbed up the bleachers toward the lone figure in the cowboy hat.

"Have a seat," he said, as she approached. "You've got your choice." His large hand indicated the empty rows around them.

"I'm trying to start a student radio show," Bitsy announced. "You have a nice voice. I could write the news, and you could read it." Bitsy's words came out in a nervous rush.

"Thanks," Billy Joe said simply. "Nobody's ever—"

"So I can count on you?" Bitsy blushed. "We can broadcast news about upcoming events—football games, concerts, rodeos."

At the mention of rodeos, Billy Joe's eyes lit up. "I—I'll think about it."

And then, to her delight, he gave her that beautiful smile and tipped his hat.

Never Love A Cowboy

Jesse DuKore

BANTAM BOOKS
TORONTO · NEW YORK · LONDON · SYDNEY

RL 6, IL age 11 and up

NEVER LOVE A COWBOY
A Bantam Book / January 1983

ISBN 0-553-23101-4

Published simultaneously in the United States and Canada

Bantam Books are published by Bantam Books, Inc. Its trademark, consisting of the words ''Bantam Books'' and the portrayal of a rooster, is Registered in U.S. Patent and Trademark Office and in other countries. Marca Registrada. Bantam Books, Inc., 666 Fifth Avenue, New York, New York 10103.

PRINTED IN THE UNITED STATES OF AMERICA

0 9 8 7 6 5 4 3 2 1

Never Love A Cowboy

Chapter One

Bitsy stood up on her toes and flung her arms around the big, beefy Irishman. She hugged him as he tousled her curly red hair.

"Sure you don't want a lift, kid?" he asked, getting into the car.

"I'm a walker!" said Bitsy staunchly.

She stood on the front porch and waved goodbye to her father. As his faded blue Ford disappeared around the corner, Bitsy gathered up her schoolbooks and her old leather bag containing stubby pencils, comb, lip gloss, and tissues. She quickly checked herself in the hallway mirror, grimaced at her unruly hair, and patted her lean, firm stomach wishing she were more curvaceous—like those tall, blond Texas beauties who were her new schoolmates.

"Seven-fifteen," she said aloud. "Let's get this show on the road!"

She strode purposefully along Red River, the curvy road that wound its way through the hills and flatland to San Jacinto High School.

It was September in Austin, Texas, and for Bitsy White, the start of a new life. After growing up in a crowded apartment building in Brooklyn, after adjusting to high school and her parents' long separation and divorce, finally Bitsy had got a break. Her father had decided to start all over again. He was a New York City policeman, and last June he had accepted a job as chief security officer with a Brooklyn electronics firm that was relocating to Austin, the capital of the Longhorn State. All during that hot, humid Brooklyn summer, Bitsy could think, talk, and dream of nothing but Texas.

Growing up on the streets of Brooklyn, Bitsy imagined the streets of Austin would be dusty and primitive. She pictured handsome young cowboys cantering by, wearing boots and spurs and white ten-gallon Stetsons. They would be tanned, their faces weathered from long days driving cattle on the range.

Now as she walked along the narrow sidewalks and quiet streets, so different from the dirt and noise of her old Brooklyn surround-

2

ings, she thought she heard the cloppety-clop-clopping of a horse's hooves. Bitsy turned around, and her heart turned over. There he was, the cowboy of her dreams. But this was no dream—this was really happening!

He was sitting high atop a brown-and-white mare, riding along Red River. The horse looked kind of old, but still it *was* a horse. And the hat was old and faded, not a gleaming Stetson. But it was the face beneath the hat that grabbed Bitsy's heart. And not just the face. It was the eyes—deep blue, beautiful, and looking straight at her. And the smile, the attitude, the twinkle in those blue eyes. He was wearing a denim jacket, a denim shirt, and denim pants.

"Hey!" he cried out. "Are you the new girl from Brooklyn?"

His boots are real cowboy boots, thought Bitsy. Not like those phony, fancy city boots. No, sir, those boots are lived in. They belong in those stirrups.

"Are you deaf?" he asked, grinning.

Bitsy took a deep breath when she realized that this real live cowboy with the smiling face was actually talking to her.

"Oh, yeah," she said.

The words barely came out. She couldn't stop swallowing hard. This is ridiculous, she told herself. I've seen guys on horses before. A

3

horse is a horse. A boy is a boy. What's the big deal?

"Yes," said Bitsy again, and couldn't think of anything else to say.

The boy's grin faded slowly.

Oh, no, thought Bitsy. This is some great start that we're off to. My first real cowboy, and I can't even talk.

But then the boy ducked his head and asked shyly, "Ever been up on a horse before?"

Before she could confess that she'd always been afraid of horses, Bitsy heard a car screech to a halt behind the old horse. From inside the shiny chrome station wagon—a relic from her father's generation—a small, pretty face was staring out at the cowboy and the city girl. Bitsy recognized her new friend, Marcia Mobley.

"Hey, Bitsy," Marcia cried out, "you going to let that cowboy pick you up? He's a dangerous flirt. Thinks all the girls are so in love with him 'cause he's crazy enough to bring a horse to school."

"Marcia," said the young man, blushing, "I'm just trying to make this new girl feel at home."

"Oh, Billy Joe, she doesn't need you for her welcome wagon. Bitsy, get in. We'll give you a ride."

Billy Joe laughed softly and shook his head. Then he waved goodbye to Bitsy.

"Well, come on in," said Marcia. "We're going to be late."

"Doesn't anybody walk in this town?"

"Are you getting in or not?" Marcia tried again.

Bitsy smiled at a blue-haired lady behind the wheel. The lady was wearing her crazy-colored hair in rollers. Bitsy wondered why she would go out like that. She thought of her own mother, who was always so carefully groomed.

"Oh, Bitsy, this is my mother," said Marcia.

"How do you do, Mrs. Mobley?"

The blue-haired lady sighed. "Is your friend getting in or not? I don't have all day."

"Come on out, Marcia," said Bitsy. "It's a great morning. Let's walk. It's good for your legs."

"Bitsy's from Brooklyn, New York," Marcia explained to her mother. The mother nodded her head, as if all Yankees were automatically weird—turning down perfectly good rides to walk in the hot sun. She leaned over so Marcia could kiss her cheek.

"See y'all later," said Mrs. Mobley.

Marcia hopped out and waved goodbye as her mother drove off. For a few seconds, Bitsy and Marcia walked along in silence. Finally, Bitsy felt she was ready to burst.

"So tell me his name already!"

5

"He's spoken for," said Marcia. "Kind of."

"Who's he engaged to—his horse?"

"His name is Billy Joe Bridges. He's from somewhere in East Texas. Really poor. Lives out that way, across the river," said Marcia, pointing. "And he's got a thing for Betty Lou Bender, Miss Conceited. We call her the Ice Queen."

"Billy Joe Bridges," said Bitsy dreamily. "What a great name."

"Hold on," cried Marcia. "You think that's a great name? That's just a plain old Texas name. And it goes—or maybe I should say it's trying to go—with Betty Lou Bender's."

"So he's not *actually* going with someone," reasoned Bitsy as she shifted her leather bag from her left to her right shoulder. "Not yet."

"Well, the Ice Queen thinks she's going to be an oil millionaire's dream girl. She pours herself into her jeans. Spends hours in the ladies' room, primping and fussing and being in love with her alabaster white skin and ruby red lips and platinum blond hair."

Marcia paused to catch her breath. As they continued walking, more cars passed them. Some were driven by parents, taking their kids to school. Some were driven by juniors and seniors. But there was only one horse, one genuine horse, and that was ridden by the one and only genuine Billy Joe Bridges, cowboy.

Marcia waved at the passing cars, pointing out the various personalities of San Jacinto High to Bitsy. There was the Tex-Mex minibus, driven by the good-looking Cesar Portillo. In the backseat was wide-eyed, oval-faced Tony Gomez, lugging his guitar wherever he went.

"Hey," shouted Cesar, "who's the cute redhead?"

"Bitsy White," shouted back Bitsy White. "Who are you?"

Cesar slowed down, surprised. "Funny accent," he said.

"You think *my* accent is funny," shouted Bitsy. "You should have heard the people in my old neighborhood. Especially the Roulettes."

"What are the Roulettes?" asked Tony curiously.

"It's a club in Brooklyn," said Bitsy. "I used to be a member. We had the best punk band in the neighborhood."

"Well, welcome to Texas," shouted Cesar.

The minibus roared away. Marcia looked at her new friend and shook her head.

"Punk band? You sure do some strange things," said Marcia. But her words flew by, and the cars flew by, and the sad little wooden houses—still a novelty to Bitsy, who grew up with big brick buildings—suddenly held no interest. All she could think of was that cowboy in denim.

"How come I've never seen him before?" asked Bitsy. "A guy on a horse would stand out, even here."

"Especially here," said Marcia. "Nobody rides horses anymore. Oh, maybe a few old-timers, up north in the Panhandle—but most cowboys today use jeeps and helicopters. Horses are for movies."

"And high school," said Bitsy. "You don't think he's crazy, do you? Why would anyone ride a horse along Red River? Can he park it— do you park a horse?—over at school?"

"You sure ask a lot of questions," said Marcia, sounding slightly annoyed. "You keep it up and we're going to start calling you the Question-Mark Kid."

So Bitsy remained silent as they approached the enormous parking lot of San Jacinto High School. A small crowd was gathered in the center of the lot. Sure enough, Bitsy could make out her cowboy, still astride his horse, patting her mane, while Cesar and Tony and a whole bunch of kids kept looking at and touching the horse. And Billy Joe was sitting tall, just as cool as a cowboy in a cigarette ad, fielding questions from his parking lot audience.

Marcia stared at Bitsy. She knew Bitsy was hooked.

"You want to go over and join the crowd?" asked Marcia.

"Not me," said Bitsy. "I don't want to be late for class."

But she couldn't resist taking a peek at the boy on the horse. She was dying to ask him all kinds of questions—about why he wore that kind of hat and why he wore those clothes and how he took care of the horse and where he got that funny accent and why he had that peculiar rhythm to his speech and that cute glint in his eye and. . . .

And there was Billy Joe Bridges waving to someone in a small, open car. The small, open car turned out to be an elegant, silver gray Mercedes convertible. A very pretty girl was taking her time getting out. She had all of Billy Joe's attention. Oh, he was still talking and patting his horse, and Tony and Cesar and the others were still hanging around—but Billy Joe was staring as hard as he could at the girl who was fixing her hair in the rearview mirror.

"Hey, Bitsy, I thought you were in such a hurry to get to class."

"Oh, yeah, Marcia, I'm coming."

But Bitsy had a funny pain in the middle of her chest; a pain she'd never felt before. She wanted to run, but she couldn't move. And she could scarcely breathe. She knew, without consciously admitting it, that she had a crush on this boy. And she also knew, in a sinking, deep-down, inside way, that she was experiencing her first pangs of jealousy. Bitsy wanted to die when the girl in the Mercedes convertible finally finished fussing with her hair and stepped out of the car.

"Hey, Betty Lou," shouted Billy Joe, "come over here and meet my horse. I'll take you for a ride."

Betty Lou very deliberately stared icily in the direction of the horse.

"Well, there she is." Marcia sneered. "Betty Lou Bender. Queen of the Junior Class."

"Oh, wow," Bitsy gasped. "She looks like a TV star."

Bitsy just knew her red hair was wilting and all out of place. She felt skinny and ugly and awkward compared to Betty Lou. At that moment Bitsy hated every single thing about herself.

"Is she Billy Joe's girl?" whispered Bitsy.

"Doesn't he wish," chortled Marcia.

Bitsy turned her attention back to Billy Joe. She couldn't take her eyes off him. Likewise, he couldn't take his eyes off Betty Lou. Bitsy turned suddenly and saw that Marcia had caught her staring.

"Don't waste your time on that dude from East Texas," she warned.

"Who says I'm wasting my time?" asked Bitsy. But in her heart of hearts, she was asking herself that same question.

Chapter Two

At twelve o'clock noon on that Monday in September, the cafeteria was noisy and crowded. Bitsy clutched her brown plastic tray, trying both to balance her lunch and to follow a fast-moving Marcia Mobley. Her friend was looking for "the music table," where Tony Gomez and all the music students hung out. Bitsy dashed after Marcia, all the while glancing around, hoping to catch a glimpse of Billy Joe.

Oh, please, she thought, let him be sitting alone. I hope he comes to his senses and realizes the Ice Queen is all wrong for him. If he gives me just half a chance, I'll let him give me a ride on his horse. I'll tell him all about the Roulettes; I'll tell him all about my father; I'll even let him meet my father. He'll love my father; my father will love *him*!

Then Bitsy knew that she was absolutely crazy, madly insane. For the first time she was insanely in love—and nothing in her life had prepared her for this magical, terrible moment.

"Bitsy, over here!"

The voice of Tony Gomez carried over the din of several hundred jabbering San Jacinto students. It took Bitsy several seconds to direct herself to the voice. She realized she had lost track of Marcia. Then she saw Tony and Marcia waving her over to a far corner. And two very cute boys stood up, grinning broadly and waving. Pretty soon, the whole table was standing and waving. Bitsy blushed a deeper red than her hair and hurried over to them. Everyone sat down and began eating.

"Bitsy White," said Marcia, "I want you to meet David Mills. Dave plays a mean guitar."

"And I sing like Willie Nelson," added Dave matter-of-factly. "He's an Austin boy."

Bitsy took a long look at this newest home-grown Texas boy. There was no one like him back up north in Brooklyn. The faces down here were different; the sounds were different; the thinking was different. Like this new kid, Dave. His hair was sandy. His face was sandy. And his body was long and lean. He reminded Bitsy a little of her cowboy. But Billy Joe was somehow more special. She sighed and wondered if being in love, or having a crush, or whatever the word was, had to be this crazy. Was every boy she met going to remind her of Billy Joe?

"And this is Specs Glassberg," said Marcia, continuing her role as hostess. "He's a fine composer. Writes words and music."

"Pleased to make your acquaintance," said the shy, chubby boy from behind enormous glasses. "I hear you're from Brooklyn." Bitsy nodded as she began eating the funny-looking food on her plate.

"I'm from Rosenberg," continued Specs. "That's just outside of Houston."

Bitsy nodded, but again, words escaped her. She had never met so many new people all at once.

"And you remember me," said Tony. "Specs and Dave and I have a group: the Wing Dings."

"Oh, yeah, the Wing Dings," said Bitsy, nodding her head as if she'd heard of them. "I used to sing with the Roulettes."

"Oh, sure," said Tony, acting as if the Roulettes were a household name. "Maybe you'd like to sing with us?"

"No," said Bitsy. "I'm retired from show business. We gave our farewell appearance at Coney Island, under the boardwalk."

"You northern girls sure are fast talkers," said Specs Glassberg.

Bitsy blushed for about the twenty-fifth time that morning. She didn't *mean* to be giving this impression, but it was so hard to know what to say to all these strangers.

She made an effort to relax and began eating her lunch. And suddenly she had something to talk about—the food, which was very different from what she was used to. She asked all about the grits and black-eyed peas and collard greens. The kids at the table were glad to tell her things. They liked talking to this eager girl who was so curious about things they took for granted.

"Boy," said Tony, "you sure ask a lot of questions."

"We're going to call her the Question-Mark Kid," volunteered Marcia.

Just then Billy Joe Bridges walked by, carrying a tray of food with one hand, as though he were holding the reins of a horse. His casual power was not lost on Bitsy White. As he surveyed the immense hall, his eyes narrowed and squinted, as if (in Bitsy's red-hot imagination) he might have been looking for a lost steer. Bitsy munched on a collard green and pondered her next move. Back home she would have thought nothing of asking Billy Joe over to her table. But, well, she *had* only met him that morning. Nevertheless . . . nevertheless. . . .

15

"Hey, Billy Joe!" she called.

Billy Joe turned around and around, as if the sound were echoing through canyons.

Marcia giggled. Olive-skinned Tony blushed. Specs looked into his hamburger.

And Dave sat back and roared with laughter. "Hey, Billy Joe," he cried out, "I think you've made yourself a new friend!"

Bitsy fixed Dave with a hard stare, which silenced him for the time being.

And then Billy Joe sauntered over and stood for a moment between Dave and Specs until they made room for him to sit between them . . . facing Bitsy.

"I'll join you for a little while," said Billy Joe. "But then I've got to be going. I'm going to the Mexicali Rodeo. It's a lot of bronco-busting and fancy riding. I figured I'd check out the competition because I want to enter every event right after graduation."

Bitsy could have listened to him forever. He sounded just like a TV cowboy—from one of those old black-and-white movies. Bitsy had thought those cowboy accents were some kind of show-business gimmick—until she had come to Texas. Marcia and the other kids had accents, and their rhythms and pronunciation of words were strange. Some of their expressions were even stranger. But Billy Joe Bridges was something else. He seemed to be a real, honest-

16

to-goodness cowboy. And he was cute and nice and shy and strong all at the same time.

"I never heard of the Mexicali Rodeo," said Dave.

"Me neither," said Specs. "You sure you didn't make it up?"

"They've put up posters downtown," said Billy Joe. "And there was a big ad in the Sunday paper."

"Wow!" said Marcia. "You actually read the Sunday paper?"

Bitsy just sat there, taking in the whole scene. She saw how cute and sensitive Tony seemed to be. Specs also seemed nice. He kept pushing his metal-framed glasses back up on his nose. All he wanted to do was talk about music: country and western and classical and when was the group going to rehearse again? And Dave just kept everything to himself and sipped his Dr Pepper. But every once in a while, he'd sneak a long, lingering look at Marcia Mobley. And every once in a while, Bitsy would sneak a long, lingering look at Billy Joe.

"Well, sure I read the paper," said Billy Joe. "Don't you? It's the only way to keep up with the important sporting events and things around town."

"I agree," said Bitsy.

"Why, thank you," said Billy Joe.

Just then Betty Lou Bender pranced by.

Bitsy shoved a chunk of rye bread into her mouth and chewed ferociously.

"Hi, Betty Lou," said Billy Joe.

How disgusting, thought Bitsy. Poor Billy Joe looks and sounds like a lovesick puppy. How can he possibly be attracted to someone just because she wears cherry red lipstick and fusses with her hair and obviously spends hours every morning in front of the mirror? Bitsy's mother used to sit by the window and look down on Flatbush Avenue, checking out everybody and saying, "There's no accounting for taste." Momma was right, thought Bitsy.

"Now, Billy Joe," purred Betty Lou, "don't forget to clap real loud today. I want to hear you cheering for me."

"Why, Betty Lou," said Marcia, in her sweetest voice, "are you going to ride one of those big bad broncos?"

"Never you mind," snapped Betty Lou. "It just so happens I'm in a very special contest. The Junior Chamber of Commerce entered me in a beauty contest that's being conducted at the rodeo."

"And that contest," said Billy Joe, to anyone at the table who would listen, "is Miss Bronco-Busting of the Year. How about that?"

"Beats me how all these events never got announced around school," said Dave.

Betty Lou flashed a quick smile and was

gone. Billy Joe took the unfinished half of his peanut butter sandwich, mumbled something, and ran off after Betty Lou.

Everyone ate in silence for a while.

"So how come nobody knew about the rodeo or the beauty contest?" Bitsy finally asked.

"You sure have a lot of questions." Marcia sighed.

"Seriously," insisted Bitsy. "How come nobody knew?" Cesar Portillo walked by, flashed a brilliant smile, and sat down in the space vacated by Billy Joe.

"Cesar—" began Bitsy.

"Bitsy—" began Cesar.

"You ever hear about the Mexicali Rodeo?" she asked.

"Sure," said Cesar. "Always wanted to see it."

"Well, it's in town," said Marcia. "Only nobody reads the Sunday papers or hangs out downtown where the posters are."

Cesar pondered this information, nodding his head. Just then, a beautiful Oriental girl walked by. Elizabeth Ho and her family were originally from Saigon.

"Elizabeth," said Cesar, "you want to go to the rodeo?"

Elizabeth smiled. Bitsy thought she seemed especially nice. She carried her good looks in a

19

relaxed manner. There was no flaunting; no showing off—unlike the Ice Queen.

"I just found out about the beauty contest," said Elizabeth, speaking impeccable English without the trace of an accent. She shrugged her shoulders.

"So how come there isn't a newspaper," asked Bitsy, "where all these events can be listed?"

"Good question," said Specs.

"Nobody reads," said Elizabeth—and she was right.

The bell sounded the end of lunch hour. Suddenly the long table was deserted. Everyone in the mammoth cafeteria began heading for the exits. Bitsy rose slowly from the table. Only Tony was still there, looking at her with his large, brown eyes.

"This school needs some help," announced Bitsy.

"Sure does." Tony grinned, then stood and joined the throng of students streaming out the door.

Bitsy consulted her schedule card, noted that her next class was physical education, and grimaced at the thought of getting into her ugly green gym suit. But then her thoughts went back to the idea that was beginning to take shape inside her head. There was definitely a gap—definitely a need for a newspaper or a radio program right here at San Jacinto High.

Later, as she changed clothes amid the crowd of jabbering girls, Bitsy began to get excited. She would make her mark on this strange, new school. What she could not admit to herself was that the real mark she wanted to make was a bull's-eye in the heart of Billy Joe Bridges.

Chapter Three

As Bitsy walked down the hallway at the end of the school day, her heart beat faster at the possibility of seeing the cowboy again. When she ran across the campus, she almost knocked two people down. She couldn't keep her head on straight or her eyes straight ahead. She was constantly turning around, eyes darting, hoping for a glimpse of Billy Joe Bridges. She looked around one last time, before setting off for her car-hopping waitressing job at a drive-in restaurant called Park 'N Pick.

As she walked, her mind kept bouncing from the boy on the horse to a picture of herself—Bitsy White, investigative reporter. Couldn't she be the driving force behind a school newspaper? Why not? Bitsy saw herself outside a stable—just herself and Billy Joe. Would she have a pad? Would she be scribbling notes while Billy Joe talked in his sweet, funny accent? Maybe she'd use a tiny microphone, holding it close to Billy Joe's inviting mouth. Bitsy felt herself tremble; found herself walking faster.

"Hey, what's your hurry?"

The soft crunch of sneakers on dry grass followed the sound of the mellow baritone voice. Bitsy turned around. A young man was running up to her. The first thing she noticed were white teeth. The next thing that caught her eye was the size of this person—Bitsy figured him to be about six-foot-four. He was breathing easily as he stopped and smiled down at her. Wow, Bitsy thought to herself, is he handsome! Not cute, not attractive, but movie-star handsome!

"Hi. I'm Beau Chapparal. Aren't you the girl from Brooklyn, the one who—?"

"Excuse me," interrupted Bitsy. "Would you mind repeating your name? Slowly."

He grinned his whiter-than-white grin, as he pushed back his wavy blond hair.

"Beau Chapparal," he repeated slowly. "What's your name?"

"Beatrice White."

Beau laughed a full-bodied laugh. It made Bitsy nervous but she didn't know why. Maybe this Beau Chapparal was too much of everything. Like the state of Texas: too big, too handsome, too open.

"Well, glad to know you, Beatrice White!"

Now Bitsy noticed he was carrying a large orange duffel bag. He nodded his head in the direction of the stadium.

"I got football practice," he said. "Want to come watch?"

"Well, actually I don't really like football," said Bitsy.

Beau's face fell, but only for a second. Then he laughed again and give Bitsy a look of amazement.

"How can you possibly live in Texas—or anywhere in the United States—and not love football? That's practically un-American," he said good-naturedly.

Bitsy smiled, then shook her head. She couldn't tell whether or not he was putting her on.

"So what made you come running after me?" asked Bitsy.

Beau cleared his throat. "Well," he said, looking just the slightest bit uncomfortable, "I'm the quarterback for the San Jacinto Steers. You do know about the Steers, don't you? And I was wondering—"

"What makes you think I know what a quarterback is?" asked Bitsy, trying to keep from giggling.

"You sure ask a lot of questions." Beau sighed. "But that's OK. I'm patient. Anyway I heard about this new Yankee girl from Brooklyn, New York. I heard she's cute and smart and she's got red, red hair. And I don't mind telling you, I wanted a chance to check you out. Now I can confirm my scouting reports. All true."

"So now am I supposed to swoon or something because the school quarter horse is—"

"That's quarter*back*," interrupted Beau. "And I'm extending an invitation, a neighborly invitation, for you to watch your school team—and your school star—in action. C'mon. What do you say?"

"I'd like to," said Bitsy honestly, "but I have to work, and I'm already late."

She clutched her books to her cardigan sweater and began to walk away. "See you later," she called over her shoulder.

"Hey," shouted Beau Chapparal. "Is it true your name is really . . . Bitsy?"

"That's what all my friends call me," she shouted back.

Beau grinned at her, waved, and marched off.

Bitsy watched him for a moment or two, and wondered why a smaller guy with a smaller voice, who was good-looking in an offbeat way, made her heart pound—and why this big, tall, handsome blond left her cold. And Bitsy thought she knew the answer. Beau was like all the good-looking boys she'd seen on television. They were all the same. They looked alike; they talked alike. Billy Joe was unique. Even if he hadn't come riding along on a horse, he would have impressed her. He was special. And she was going to make him sit up and take notice!

Twenty minutes later, Bitsy had changed into her uniform—an orange-and-white western shirt, orange-and-white bandanna, and a smaller version of an orange-and-white Mexican sombrero, big enough to block out the afternoon sun but small enough not to get knocked off every time she leaned toward a customer.

Park 'N Pick was a Tex-Mex (Texas-Mexican) operation that featured chiliburgers, tacoburgers, tortillaburgers, and also plain, ordinary hamburgers. Bitsy worked there every afternoon after school, from three to six. She also worked Saturday mornings and some Saturday afternoons. Between five and six, Monday through Friday, work was slow enough so Bitsy had time to become friends with a waitress named Sue Ann Jones.

Bitsy liked Sue Ann, who had dropped out of high school at sixteen in order to help support her five younger sisters and brothers. She admired Sue Ann's sense of loyalty and responsibility to her family, especially considering that her father had simply disappeared last winter.

From the moment Bitsy had come to work, speaking in her colorful Brooklyn accent, questioning her uniform, and laughing at the sombreros, she and Sue Ann had hit it off. Bitsy was a great help to Sue Ann during rush hours, and during the slow periods the two girls had plenty of time to talk and get to know one another.

On this particular Monday, though, Bitsy was lost in thought. She and Sue Ann sat on high stools near the food counter, their sombreros tilted back on their heads.

"You sure are happy," Sue Ann commented jokingly to Bitsy. "Is today your birthday or something?"

"No."

They sat silently for a moment, looking out at the empty parking lot.

"Well, don't bend my ear." Sue Ann smiled. "Come on. What's up?"

Bitsy sighed. Then she looked at her friend and sighed again.

"Bitsy met a boy!" Sue Ann guessed. She let out a big laugh.

"Bitsy, you're a devil," said Sue Ann. "Four weeks in a new city and already you're taking over. Tell me all the dirt."

"No dirt," said Bitsy airily. "Not much to tell."

"I'll bet," said Sue Ann. "When are you seeing him again?"

Bitsy thought for a moment. "Oh, probably tomorrow morning," she said.

Sue Ann laughed again, then slapped her thigh emphatically. "Bitsy met a boy at school, and she's got a terrible crush on him, and he doesn't know she's alive, and she doesn't know what to say or what to do or—"

A big, dirty Cadillac convertible screeched to a halt, honking its horn at the same time.

"I'll get it," called Bitsy, running out the door.

A huge German shepherd leaned forward from the backseat as Bitsy hooked a tray onto the open window. The driver looked like no one Bitsy had ever seen before. He was about thirty years old, she figured, with a crew cut and the pinkest face imaginable. But what was most amazing was the man's size. He was the fattest man she had ever seen. He spread out all across the front seat. Only a very skinny person could have sat up front next to him. And he must have been tall because, even with the seat pushed back, the steering wheel was up against his bulging belly.

"May I take your order?" asked Bitsy.

The man smiled shyly, then proceeded to order the double chiliburger, the tacoburger, the tortillaburger, and the enchiladaburger. And a cup of tea. With lemon.

"Any dessert?" asked Bitsy. She couldn't believe the words coming out of her mouth, but then again, Bitsy couldn't believe the food order coming out of the man's mouth. He laughed a gentle, understanding laugh.

"No, ma'am," he said. "Fellow's got to know his limits; got to know when to walk away. Or drive away, as the case may be."

The German shepherd barked, as if agreeing with his master. Bitsy jumped back, almost losing her order pad and pencil. But she recovered enough to step forward gingerly and clear her throat.

"Anything for the dog?" she asked.

The man shook his head. "Pluto eats enough for a pride of lions. I think maybe I spoiled him."

"Be right back," said Bitsy.

She walked quickly to the food counter and gave her order to the cook. While she waited, she wondered what it was about this state of Texas, where everything really was bigger. Maybe not better, but certainly bigger.

Fifteen minutes later, Bitsy and Sue Ann were seated at tables outside, their sombreros tilted forward on their heads. Bitsy had opened her heart to Sun Ann, who proved to be the good friend she was simply by listening and being sympathetic.

"I used to party all the time back in Brooklyn," confessed Bitsy. "But I never had a special boyfriend. I mean, there were some nice guys, some cute guys, but deep down I was always asking myself, 'Is this all there is?' Somehow, even when I was thirteen and fourteen and fifteen, I knew there had to be something more, someone really special. This guy on the horse just might be the someone for me. I wish you could meet him. Now what do I do?"

"I sure wish I had your problem," said Sue Ann. "I never get to meet any of those cute schoolboys. By the time Saturday night comes around, I just want to curl up and go to sleep all the way to Monday."

Just then, a pickup truck, a motorcycle, and three station wagons all converged on Park 'N Pick at the same time.

"Carhops, man your posts," shouted Sue Ann.

"Wrong!" shouted back Bitsy. "It's 'person your posts.' "

"Whatever it is, y'all better get crackin'!"

Bitsy loved to hear Sue Ann's thick Texas accent. But, she thought, the best sound in the world was the East Texas voice of Billy Joe Bridges. Bitsy just couldn't stop thinking about him. She would have to find a way to make him notice her and like her.

"Bitsy's got that lovin' look again," whispered Sue Ann, scooping up a tray of chiliburgers and sodas.

Oh, no, thought Bitsy. If Sue Ann can see right through me, then everybody probably can. This is no way to start a new life!

But somewhere deep inside, Ms. Beatrice "Bitsy" White was secretly a little bit pleased. She was in love for the first time, with all the problems of "love at first sight," and wasn't heartache always a part of romance?

Chapter Four

It was almost six o'clock. The sky was an enormous canvas of red sun and streaks and wisps of pink clouds. Bitsy was looking forward to kicking off her boots and just relaxing. She was so tired she could hardly move. But before she could throw her sombrero, Frisbee-style, onto the wire hook in the dressing room, the big voice of Sue Ann Jones called out: "You got the last customer, kid. Looks like a big tip."

Bitsy dragged her feet to the parking lot, putting on her last cheery smile of the day. She gasped when she recognized her communications teacher slumped against the wheel of an old Pinto.

Mr. Gonzales was one of Bitsy's more memorable teachers. He taught lively, interesting classes, but he seemed to hold himself slightly apart from his students, running a strict, tightly disciplined, and very controlled classroom. Which was why Bitsy was now surprised to find him pleading unsuccessfully with his five-year-old son to eat something. Anything!

"Hello, Mr. Gonzales. I'm Beatrice White. Bitsy. I'm in your communications class."

Mr. Gonzales took off his thick horn-rimmed glasses, wiped his moist forehead with a handkerchief, and scratched his head.

"Oh, yes. Bitsy. Well, maybe you can communicate with my five-year-old son. John, this is Bitsy. She's going to bring you some goodies."

"What would you like, John?" asked Bitsy uncertainly.

The little boy with the big brown eyes began to cry.

Mr. Gonzales took out his handkerchief again and tried to wipe away the tears. "Shhh, John," he soothed. "This nice young lady has a big surprise for you. A real tasty burger and a real tasty milk shake. Chocolate!"

"I want fries!" sobbed the boy. "I want fries and a Coke and Twinkies."

Mr. Gonzales looked like a defeated man.

He shrugged his shoulders as Bitsy waited patiently, her pencil poised.

"That's all junk food, Mr. Gonzales," said Bitsy. "Can't I get him something more nutritious?"

"Sure you can," said the teacher, "but I'll have a crying child on my hands all night long."

"How about a compromise?" suggested Bitsy. "If you eat a hamburger, John, you can have a Coke with it."

John considered this for a full minute and finally agreed.

"Whew! Thanks," said Mr. Gonzales. "And make that two orders."

Maybe it was the time of day. Maybe it was because Bitsy felt so tired. Maybe it was just the ridiculous situation of a capable teacher turning into a frantic father. Or maybe it was a combination of everything that had happened that day. But Bitsy found herself relaxed and open to new ideas. As she waited for the food order to be prepared, the jumble of events and impressions that had been churning inside her all fell into place. She felt serene. Her head was clear. And as she carried Mr. Gonzales's order to him and set it down on the tray, she suddenly cried, "I have it, Mr. Gonzales, I have it!"

"Huh?"

"What our school needs—" Bitsy began, interrupting Mr. Gonzales's dinner. She paused dramatically, so the harried parent could collect himself. "What our school needs is a radio news show, operated by the students and for the students. I think it could be a neat way to teach the kids about, well, radio and news—and how to write it and how to speak it or say it or whatever you do with it. And it would be performing a public service. We can have loudspeakers in the cafeteria and in the school corridors. And we can call it—"

Mr. Gonzales continued to eat. John was examining a bit of hamburger, holding it up to his nose so he could sniff it and pick it apart at the same time.

Bitsy took a deep breath and continued. "We can call it . . . KALL. K-A-L-L. I just found out—I guess it was in your class—that stations west of the Mississippi have call letters starting with K. So I think it would be an excellent idea to call it KALL."

There was a long silence. Bitsy knew her teacher wanted to be left in peace, but she didn't care. She saw herself alone in a studio with Billy Joe Bridges, with only a microphone between them. She would ask him everything about his life in East Texas. He would tell all, answering in his slow, colorful drawl. Then she imagined herself broadcasting all kinds of news and school and social events. Her voice would echo through the halls and the cafeteria of San Jacinto High. And then, on a night not too far away, she would be home studying, and the telephone would ring. She would run to pick it up. And she'd hear the voice of Billy Joe Bridges, asking her out for a Saturday night date.

The raspy voice of Robert Gonzales broke her delightful reverie. "That's really interesting. But let's talk about it tomorrow."

"OK, sure," Bitsy said, then walked away. "I don't care what he says," she mumbled. "I know it's a good idea—a *great* idea. I just have to tell him about it at the proper time."

Ten minutes later, Bitsy and Sue Ann were walking home. Bitsy was pleased that Sue Ann was a neighbor, if living one mile apart could be considered neighborly. Sue Ann boasted that a mile in Texas was just a hop, skip, and a jump.

They reached Red River, and from somewhere in the distance Bitsy heard a loud clicking sound.

"Hey, what's that?" she asked.

"What?"

"That funny, click-click-clickety sound. Sounds sort of like a cricket, only louder."

Sue Ann roared with laughter. Bitsy laughed along with Sue Ann, even though she didn't know what was so funny.

"Come on already," cried Bitsy. "What's so funny?"

"Those *are* crickets. Don't you people even have crickets in Brooklyn? Why, I'll bet you've never seen a cow. Do you know what a cow or a cricket or a bull or a rattlesnake looks like?"

"Well, of course, I've seen cows and bulls—outside Brooklyn, I mean. And I'd recognize a rattlesnake from pictures and TV, but I'm not sure I'd know a cricket if I fell over one."

"You don't *fall* over a cricket!" Sue Ann giggled. "They're just little insects."

"Yeah, I know," said Bitsy, turning away from the vista below. "But these Texas crickets sure make a lot of noise."

In fact, Bitsy noticed, the noise from the crickets was getting louder and louder. Suddenly she looked down. They were surrounded by *hundreds* of the little, dark insects. And a lot of them weren't so little. Bitsy couldn't walk without stepping on them. She began to tremble with fear. There was no way to walk without feeling the crunch. Bitsy froze. Sue Ann merely stepped out into the street.

"This always happens this time of year," she explained. "It's because of the humidity. Come on, Bitsy. They don't bite."

"I'm afraid to move," cried Bitsy. "There must be thousands of them. They're going to crawl up my legs!"

"No, they're not," said Sue Ann impatiently. "Now let's go. I've got to get dinner on the table."

"Go on ahead," shouted Bitsy. "I'll find a way out. I just don't want them in my hair. Oh, no! Tell them to shut up already. Shut up, crickets! Get out of my way!"

Sue Ann stood there in the street, laughing at her new friend, who could be so scared by a bunch of clicking crickets.

Just then, a dusty black pickup truck screeched to a halt behind Sue Ann. The back of the truck was filled with kindling wood and logs. In the front seat, a grimy-faced young man looked out the window and laughed at the pretty redhead.

"Looks like you're stranded," he said pleasantly. He patted the back of his neck with a dirty red handkerchief, then wiped the grime off his forehead.

Bitsy recognized him immediately. Billy Joe Bridges! She wanted to cry, for fear, for relief; the tears began streaming down her cheeks so fast they surprised everyone, especially herself. She smiled a helpless smile, even managed a little laugh and a shrug of the shoulders—but her feet refused to move.

Billy Joe sensed immediately what the problem was. "Be right there," he shouted.

"Hey, Bitsy," said Sue Ann. "Looks like y'all got yourself a knight in dirty armor."

"Well," said Billy Joe, "it's good honest dirt. I've been working upriver, getting wood for my stove. It's going to be a cold winter. Big norther's going to be coming down next month."

"Please," interrupted Bitsy. "Could you do the weather report some other time?"

Billy Joe nodded. "You look like you could use some help," he said, getting out of his truck.

"I see you're in good hands," Sue Ann said, then winked at Bitsy. "I'll see you tomorrow." She crossed the street, then turned to wave—at the precise moment Billy Joe reached out his hand and led Bitsy out of the mass of crawling creatures. Sue Ann smiled and walked away quickly.

If she had waited another second, she would have seen Billy Joe suddenly and dramatically sweep Bitsy off her feet and carry her into the street and around to the side of the pickup truck, where he gently put her down.

"Thanks." Bitsy spoke in a quiet, choked voice. Being so close so suddenly to this boy left her feeling breathless and very self-conscious. He had been so understanding, so considerate—literally sweeping her off her feet and not laughing at her—and all she could do was barely whisper, "Thanks." Now they were standing together, out on the street, while the engine of the pickup truck purred away in neutral.

"You have a horse *and* a truck," Bitsy finally managed to say.

"Yep. But I don't usually ride my horse to school. I rode her just for the rodeo," said Billy Joe. "It was part of my costume."

"Costume?"

"Sure. Don't you wear different outfits for different occasions?"

"Yes."

"Well, a rodeo is a different occasion," explained Billy Joe. "It calls for a horse, a big, old cowboy hat, and a fancy bandanna."

"Bandanna?" asked Bitsy. "Is that like a kerchief?" She looked up at the red bandanna around his neck. He still had his denim outfit on and those great old boots.

Billy Joe nodded.

"How was the rodeo?" asked Bitsy politely.

He shrugged, then turned away, placing a big hand on the door. His body suddenly looked awkward and tense. But then he turned back around and managed a smile.

"Can I give you a lift?" he asked, avoiding her question.

"Sure," said Bitsy. "I'm only another couple of blocks down the street. Well, maybe it's seven or eight blocks."

He held the door open, then helped her up and into the truck, holding out his hand in a gallant, old-fashioned manner. Bitsy smiled shyly as she took it and got inside the truck. She wished she could stay there holding his hand forever, but it lasted only a moment. Billy Joe walked around the truck, kicked a few crickets away, and jumped inside the cabin.

"Straight down Red River?" he asked.

"Yes, please. Thank you."

Bitsy didn't know what to say as Billy Joe drove along. She was thrilled he had "saved" her—though a bit embarrassed that she had been so frightened of some noisy little insects. She was also curious about the rodeo. Why didn't he want to talk about it? Bitsy glanced sideways at him. He looked so serious, almost sad.

"This is my house," said Bitsy.

"OK."

As Bitsy sat beside Billy Joe, there were so many questions she wanted to ask him. Should she invite him in for a soda? Should she ask him about the rodeo? About the truck? About the dirt on his hands and face? About her idea for a radio news show? But before she could open her mouth, Billy Joe had switched off the engine, jumped out of the cabin, run around the front of the pickup truck, and opened the passenger door.

"I'm sorry," said Bitsy. "I wasn't waiting for you to open the door for me. I could have opened it."

Billy Joe stood there stiffly, his face noticeably red even in the early evening darkness.

"A gentleman always opens a door for a lady," he said.

"Well, thank you."

Bitsy took his proffered hand, holding it as she jumped onto the sidewalk. There was a light on in the small wooden house. The blue Ford was in the driveway.

"Like to come in for a soda?" she asked.

"I—I—better not," he said uncomfortably. "It's supper time."

"Didn't you go to the rodeo?" Bitsy blurted out, overcome by curiosity.

He sighed. Then he shoved his hands into the pockets of his jeans. The heel of his boot dug into the soil that surrounded the elm tree.

"Actually, I didn't have the money," he confessed.

"I could have lent you some money," said Bitsy. "I'm working over at Park 'N Pick."

"You can't lend money to a stranger," said Billy Joe.

"You're not a stranger," said Bitsy.

"Oh, yes, I am. You hardly know me."

Bitsy nodded her head. But Billy Joe laughed, and she knew he was teasing her a little.

"I love your horse," she said.

"Thanks," said Billy Joe.

Bitsy thought, quite possibly, that she would scream. It would be a scream that would knock down the elm tree, the wooden house, and Billy Joe Bridges. She wanted to kiss him—right then and there. She wanted *him* to kiss *her*. But they stood under the branches of the elm tree as the first evening star appeared in the Texas sky, saying nothing, doing nothing. His hands were thrust deep inside the pockets of his jeans. She was holding a notebook and a couple of textbooks against her stomach, shifting the weight of her body from her left side to her right side, and back again.

"Thanks for saving my life," said Bitsy.

"Aw, it was nothing," said Billy Joe. "Crickets are pretty harmless."

"I guess so."

And then, without so much as a "goodbye" or a "see you later," he jumped back up into the truck, slid behind the wheel, and started the engine. A moment later, the wooden logs and branches were shaking and rattling as the truck sped away. Bitsy just stood there, looking at the spot where the pickup truck had been.

"Want to come inside?" she asked the darkness. "I'll fix you dinner. I'll fix you anything you want. Only, *please*, let me get to know you."

The only reply was the faraway chirping of the crickets. Bitsy sighed heavily and strode into the house. Her father was in the kitchen, concentrating on basting a chicken. She kissed his cheek, then dropped her books heavily onto the kitchen table.

"Who was the boy?"

Bitsy made a face as she shook her head at him. "Oh, Dad! Just a friend, that's all."

Mr. White left the chicken for a moment. He eyed Bitsy seriously. "I wish you'd let me in on your new life sometime, sweetie," he said. "I hate to remind you, but eventually I have to answer to your mother about you. By the way, you got a card from her today. It's on the table."

Bitsy casually picked up the card and sank down in a chair to read its few words:

Dearest Bitsy,

I think about you every day and miss you. All of this is a lot tougher than I

thought it would be, but you know I have
to try. How are you, baby?

Love,
Mom

For a moment Bitsy's eyes filled with tears.
How could her mother have just left her? Who
was the real baby—Bitsy or Belinda White? After
the divorce, Belinda had taken her share of the
money from the settlement and gone to Europe,
practically like a teenager running away from
home. Phrases in her mother's voice ran through
Bitsy's mind: "I married your father when I was
only nineteen. . . . I've always been hungry to
travel. . . . I've got to get off by myself and
discover who I am. . . . I'll always love you, my
Bitsy, and I'll be back, and we can be the best of
friends, sisters. . . . I've found Italy, and I'm
staying for a while, studying Latin and paint-
ing. . . . I'm counting on you, babe, to be a
star!"

Every week a postcard came for Bitsy, but
she stubbornly refused to answer them. She
was as determined about this as she was about
everything else in her life. "If she wants to hear
from me," said Bitsy, "she can just show up
here!"

Bitsy's father tried to keep his ex-wife in-
formed of Bitsy's welfare, but sometimes Bitsy
could be very closemouthed.

Now, as Bitsy came out of her reverie about her mother, she saw him looking at her with concern.

"You OK, kiddo?" he asked softly. "She really does love you, you know."

"Oh, Dad, I love you so much!" cried Bitsy. "But right now I need to be alone."

Chapter Five

At noon on the following day, Bitsy was marching determinedly along the crowded corridors of San Jacinto High. Her thoughts, for once, were not about Billy Joe Bridges. The object of her undivided attention was her communications teacher, Mr. Gonzales.

"Hey, pretty girl, where are you going?"

The rich baritone voice belonged to Beau Chapparal. He was wearing the orange-and-white team jacket of the San Jacinto Steers. Bitsy had to admit he looked good.

"Hey, slow down," said Beau, running to keep up with fast-moving Bitsy. "You better come watch me play this coming Saturday. I'll save you a seat right on the fifty-yard line. You can

47

wave to me as I come running off the field, after I've thrown a forty-yard touchdown pass."

Bitsy's first thought was, why couldn't Billy Joe invite me to his sporting event? Then she remembered why—Billy Joe hadn't even gone to *his* sporting event.

"I have to work on Saturday," explained Bitsy.

Beau started to turn away, shaking his head in disbelief that any girl could resist the charms and good looks of the number-one quarterback. Then Bitsy grabbed him by the sleeve of his jacket.

"Beau, how would you feel about being interviewed?"

"Huh?"

Bitsy tugged at his sleeve jacket, pulling him against the blue wall of the corridor and out of the path of three galloping sophomore boys.

"Beau, if I were to do an interview with you—for a radio show—and you had a chance to be heard all through these halls and down in the cafeteria and maybe even on car radios . . . how would you feel?"

Beau slumped against the wall, a sheepish grin on his face. Two worry lines appeared across his brow.

Oh, no, thought Bitsy. Now I've got to wait while the Great Thinker ponders this problem.

But I do need all the ammunition I can get, and if this all-star, all Texas, all around BMOC goes along with my program, maybe Mr. Gonzales will say yes. And if Mr. Gonzales says yes, maybe Billy Joe will say yes. So come on, football star, let's get moving!

"Well now, Bitsy. . . ."

"Yes?"

"You really think I could do that?"

"Sure," said Bitsy. "You just talk like you're talking now, and you'll sound fine. Talk naturally. It'll be easy."

"And what am I going to talk about? I guess I know some jokes. And my buddies tell me I can sing kind of like—"

"No, no," said Bitsy quickly. "You won't have to sing or tell funny stories. All you have to do is answer some questions about football and school and what you like to do on a date and—"

Beau burst out laughing. "I can't talk like that in public," he insisted.

"Oh, come on, Beau, I just want to ask you a bunch of questions. Just a regular interview. So if I get permission to do a radio show, could I interview you?"

"Well, OK. For you, OK."

"That means yes?" asked Bitsy.

"That means yes!" said Beau.

Bitsy took off down the hallway, dodging through the crowd like a football player. Two minutes later she was standing, panting, in front of the teachers' lounge. Bitsy adjusted her navy blue skirt, made sure her pink-and-white-striped blouse was tucked in all around, and straightened her blazer. Then she entered the cold, formal room. In a far corner, Robert Gonzales was sitting in a straight-backed chair facing the window. As his eyes squinted in the noonday sun, he reached down to a brown paper bag at his feet. Bitsy watched, fascinated and afraid. She'd never been inside a teachers' lounge, and she wondered if a stern voice would tell her to leave. Two women teachers were sitting at a long table. They were also opening brown paper bags. As sandwiches and fresh fruit emerged from the bags, Bitsy felt embarrassed. She turned back to Mr. Gonzales, who was now munching on a sandwich. Every minute or so, he would place the sandwich on his lap and then reach down to pick up a container of steaming coffee. Bitsy felt her legs shaking. She knew she was intruding. But there was no going back.

"Hi, Mr. Gonzales."

All three teachers turned around. Mr. Gonzales's mouth was bulging, like a chipmunk's that was storing food for the winter. He slowly finished chewing his mouthful of food. Finally, after a long swallow, he spoke.

"Bitsy, right? Thanks for helping me out

50

last night. John actually said he liked the hamburger."

"Oh, I'm glad I could help out. . . . Listen, I'm sorry for interrupting your lunch," said Bitsy. "I didn't want to talk to you after class because there just wasn't time, and I didn't know what to say but. . . ."

The two female teachers returned to their lunch and conversation as soon as they saw Robert Gonzales handling this student intrusion. Bitsy shifted her weight from her right leg to her left, almost letting her books slip to the floor. But she retrieved them in time and took a deep breath.

"I have an idea, Mr. Gonzales. I think what this school needs—"

"Miss White. You've been here all of four weeks, and you're going to tell me what this school needs? Ever hear of the expression *carpetbagger*? That was an old post-Civil War expression. It was used by southerners to describe those northerners, salesmen, who'd journey through the South and the Southwest with a carpetbag—a piece of luggage—filled with all kinds of clothes and medicine and what have you. They would tell their would-be customers they had bargains galore, right inside their rolled-up carpetbags. Usually, the salesmen were run out of town. Carpetbaggers were not popular people."

Bitsy was getting angry. Her impression of Mr. Gonzales had taken a sharp turn for the worse. He was no mind reader and had no right to assume he knew what she was going to say. But she held her tongue and counted to ten, slowly. Her father had taught Bitsy that lesson.

"Mr. Gonzales," she said carefully, "I'd like your advice about starting that radio news show for the students."

He sighed heavily and put down his sandwich. He remained silent while he chewed. It seemed to Bitsy he pondered her words for an unusually long time.

"Do you know what's involved in this kind of project?" he asked.

"No, sir," she said, respectfully. "That's why I wanted to discuss it with you. And I knew there wouldn't be time after class."

Mr. Gonzales studied her face. It seemed to Bitsy he might have been counting the freckles around her cheekbones.

"Sit down," he said finally. "Tell me your ideas."

Bitsy breathed a long sigh and collapsed into the straight-backed chair Mr. Gonzales pulled over.

"Well," she began, "I think it would be really great if this school could be kept up to date on all local events, both in school and on the outside. . . . You know, in the city of Austin?"

"Go on. I know what 'outside' means."

"Now, if we could set up a daily program— maybe five minutes in the morning, or five minutes at lunchtime—with weather reports, social events, school events, and community events, maybe there would be a way to broadcast it in the cafeteria and the hallways. Oh yeah, and maybe on car radios? I don't know. What do you think?"

"The local station might go for the idea if we did it once a week," said Mr. Gonzales. "They probably wouldn't be too interested in school events but . . . well, do you have any other ideas?"

Bitsy felt herself getting excited. She knew she had the teacher hooked, so she deliberately took a long moment before speaking again.

"An interview program!" she announced. "I already spoke to Beau Chapparal, the football player, and he said he was willing to be interviewed. I figure I could get all kinds of school celebrities and—"

"Well, Bitsy, I don't like to sound negative, but I honestly don't know if there will be enough student interest. Beau Chapparal does not represent the student body. Now I'm not saying it's a bad idea. It's—well, it's really a good idea. But most kids at San Jacinto are just interested in sports, watching TV, listening to music, and dating. Most of the students don't have much curiosity about anything except what's happening on Friday night."

"But isn't that enough?" asked Bitsy. "We can *tell* them what's happening—everywhere. Maybe do special news stories: exposés, human interest. Right?"

"OK, but you can't run a radio program all by yourself. I know you can't. I tried. When I was in high school." He smiled helplessly. "Tell you what," he said finally. "If you can get some student support—that is, participation—come back and see me. If the students are for it, I'll be your advisor. Fair enough?"

Bitsy stood up. She straightened her back, clutched her schoolbooks, and nodded once, emphatically.

"OK," she said. "Fair enough."

She walked slowly out of the teachers' lounge. Lunch period would be over in fifteen minutes. She wasn't hungry, but she made her way down to the basement, hoping to find some interested students in the cafeteria. When she arrived, the cavernous room was half empty.

She headed straight for the music table. Marcia Mobley was gulping down a glass of milk, and Tony and Cesar had their heads buried in their notebooks. Specs and Dave and Billy Joe were nowhere to be seen. As Bitsy approached, Marcia stood up quickly and headed for the exit.

"Marcia!"

Bitsy's voice carried the length of the cafeteria. Marcia deposited her empty glass on the plastic rack and spun around, then grinned when she saw Bitsy. Even Tony and Cesar looked up from their books.

"Hey," shouted back Cesar, as he stretched his muscular frame. "Does everybody from Brooklyn have a loud voice?"

"Yeah," returned Bitsy. "That comes from spending time in the subways. You have to shout to be heard."

Cesar just shook his head, then went back to his notebooks.

Bitsy grabbed Marcia's arm. "I've got to talk to you," she said. "Big news."

"Billy Joe just asked you out," shot back Marcia.

Now it was Bitsy's turn to get embarrassed. Still, she pulled Marcia out of the cafeteria. They headed up the stairs and out into the street. All the while, Bitsy was telling Marcia about KALL. Marcia didn't seem to be listening. She sat on the steps and watched the cars go by, occasionally nodding but seeming to be very far away. Finally, Bitsy stopped speaking. She sat there, looking at her loafers. Somehow, her new life in Austin had lost some of its luster and excitement. Miss Marcia Mobley looked like she couldn't have cared less about KALL or Billy Joe or anything.

"So now let me see if I understand you properly," said Marcia finally. "You're going to report on social events."

"Yeah," said Bitsy snappishly.

"You're going to interview Beau Chapparal."

"That's the idea," said Bitsy.

"And where does Billy Joe come in?"

"I don't know," said Bitsy. "I figured maybe I'd interview him. You know, growing up in East Texas. Being a cowboy and all that."

"Well, Bitsy Beatrice White," said Marcia, "Billy Joe's no more a cowboy than I am. I mean, he looks like one. And he can ride a horse. But that doesn't make him a cowboy. I'll tell you what I think."

"What?" Bitsy sighed.

"I think you just ought to find Billy Joe Bridges and tell him what you told me. Then tell him that he'd make one fine reporter. And he'll probably jump for joy. First time anyone ever offered him anything important. Tell him he can do his own interviews. Let him interview an old cowboy. Or some old rodeo star. He'll love it."

Marcia's voice dropped to a low whisper. "And maybe," she continued, "he'll love you."

Bitsy couldn't believe the words coming out of her friend's mouth. Then she knew, deep down, that Marcia was a real friend after all. She clapped her hands.

"Marcia, your idea is terrific, really terrific!" She was so excited at the prospect that she let out a whoop. For the time being, Bitsy's only problem was how to make Billy Joe an offer he couldn't possibly turn down. Even if he weren't a genuine cowboy—according to Marcia Mobley—Bitsy would make him a genuine reporter—and maybe a genuine boyfriend.

Chapter Six

So where was Billy Joe Bridges? Bitsy had only one class that afternoon, her favorite American history. But her mind was so distracted, so filled with the face of Billy Joe, she couldn't concentrate on Ms. Bagby's words. Certainly Bitsy was interested in the War of 1812, but she was also racing ahead with her own campaign, her own strategy. She saw herself and Billy Joe at KALL, spreading the news, highlighting the events for all the kids to hear and share. The War of 1812 dragged on and on. Finally, it was two o'clock. Bitsy had one hour to track down her cowboy.

There was no horse in the parking lot, nor an old, beat-up pickup truck. There was, however, a shiny white Chevette. And tall, blond, handsome Beau Chapparal was leaning against the door. Beau waved easily as Bitsy walked toward him. He looked as if he had been waiting for her.

"What took you so long?" he asked, almost too casually.

"What do you mean?"

"You don't want to miss football practice," said Beau. "Part of the Steers' tradition is Tuesday afternoon—Student Rootin' Day. It gets everybody fired up for the game on Saturday. I thought you knew all about it. I mean, you have been here four weeks."

"Your sarcasm is noted, *Mister* Chapparal," said Bitsy. "I can't go to practice, but if you're driving to the ball field—"

"It's called a stadium," interrupted Beau.

"Stadium, playground, Astrodome, whatever you want to call it, I'll ride with you. It's on the way to Park 'N Pick. I have to work this afternoon." With a great flourish, Beau ran around to the far side of the car, opened the door for her, allowed her to enter, and closed the door with a loud slam.

On the way to the stadium, Beau talked on and on about how good the team was and how good he was, and why didn't she take off from work and just hang out with the other kids and watch him practice.

Bitsy listened. But she was thinking that Beau seemed so childish. Nice, but childish. If a young lady didn't fall all over his feet, he would get petulant and angry.

He put one big arm around his passenger's imitation cowhide seat. Kind of early in the day to get romantic, thought Bitsy. She was glad to be annoyed at him. Otherwise, she might be nervous—trapped in a Chevette with a big-deal quarterback. But Bitsy's annoyance turned to elation as the car started to pass the stadium driveway. In the parking lot was that rusty, beat-up pickup truck with a few stray wooden logs peeking out of the back. Billy Joe would be in the crowd!

"Beau, I think I'll watch you for a while after all," announced Bitsy. "I've still got time before work. May as well learn something about football, as long as I'm in football country and as long as I'm getting lifts from a football hero."

"Well," said Beau, "I don't know that I'm a *hero. . . .*"

Bitsy was so excited to have found Billy Joe, she let herself be generous. "I'll bet you *are* a hero," she said. "This'll be fine, right over here."

The Chevette came to a stop alongside the old pickup truck.

"Hey," said Beau. "Don't take your eyes off me. I'll be waving to you."

"And I'll wave back," promised Bitsy. "But I do have to get to work."

"Don't worry. It's a short walk from here. Hey, I'll get you a ticket for the game on Saturday. We're playing Trinity. They're a tough team. From San Antonio."

Beau went to get his equipment bag out of the backseat. Already, his mind was starting to zero in on football. Bitsy opened her own door, let herself out, and looked around for the entrance to the grandstand.

"I work on Saturday morning," said Bitsy. "And if we're busy, I have to stick around in the afternoon."

"See you Saturday," shouted Beau. He waved goodbye and was gone.

Beau means well, thought Bitsy, but no girl alive, at least in Austin, is going to win him. Beau is going steady with a football. Everything else is second place.

As she walked through the large entranceway, Bitsy reflected on her new social life. She already liked the boys and girls of San Jacinto much more than most of the Roulettes and the students at her old school, Erasmus Hall. The pain of her parents' divorce had made her glad to leave everything in Brooklyn. She knew that Marcia Mobley and Sue Ann Jones were going to be good, solid friends. And the guys at the music table—Specs, Tony, Dave—were genuinely warm and friendly. Cesar Portillo was handsome and intelligent; any of the Roulettes would have grabbed him in a minute. Beau was sweet; simple but sweet, for all his cockiness. But the guy who set her heart beating a mile a minute, and who didn't even know it, was sitting somewhere up there on a long bench, wearing an old hat and old boots, his beautiful blue eyes squinting in the Texas sun.

Bitsy climbed several flights of concrete stairs and came out, not under a Texas sun, but into an overcast, gray afternoon. Several clusters of dedicated football fans were standing around the fifty-yard line. Where was he? As Bitsy grew accustomed to the mammoth grandstand, she turned around, looked up and up and . . . there was a lonely, blue-denimed figure way up in the last row, at the far corner, beyond the goal posts.

Bitsy began the long climb up to the last row of the stadium. A strong wind was blowing up there, causing the flags to flap and snap loudly. The one flag that stood alone had a single white star in its blue center. This was the state flag of Texas—the Lone Star State. Other flags indicated rival high schools. By the time Bitsy got to the top row, the wind was actually howling. She looked over the iron railing to the parking lot and below. Suddenly her legs were trembling. Oh, wow, she thought. One stiff gust of wind, and I'll be flying over the top; this is not such a hot idea. And what am I doing, running after some guy who doesn't even know I'm alive?

"Oh, stop feeling sorry for yourself, Beatrice White," shouted Bitsy into the wind.

She put her head down to buck the strong wind and marched resolutely along the top row, her eyes smarting with tears from the wind. As she got closer to the lone figure, Bitsy saw he had moved down a few rows.

"Billy Joe!" she shouted.

He turned around but did not immediately recognize her. Then Bitsy realized how windswept she must look. She brushed her hair out of her face, and Billy Joe nodded in recognition.

"Have a seat," he said. "You got your choice." His large hand indicated the empty rows around them.

But Bitsy's eyes were only for the boy in the old cowboy boots.

"Getting cold," he volunteered. "Shouldn't have any trouble with crickets."

"But if I do," said Bitsy, "I'll call you. OK?"

Billy Joe grinned charmingly.

Bitsy started to sit down next to him, then changed her mind and let a space remain between them. His eyes were directed toward the goal posts. Some kind of activity was going on down there. Bitsy wiped the cold tears from her eyes and focused on the playing field.

"Who are all those people in the orange sweaters?" she asked.

"Cheerleaders," said Billy Joe, matter-of-factly. "Oh yeah, and some majorettes. Baton twirlers and all that."

Bitsy focused on the orange sweaters and white boots. Each girl was prettier than the next. Bitsy recognized Elizabeth Ho, her long, dark hair falling backward, her back arched, as she twirled a red, white, and blue baton. She dropped it, then scooped it up, then dropped it again. About ten yards away from Elizabeth was another beauty. She seemed to be doing calisthenics. She kept jumping, kicking her legs, and raising her arms at the same time. It was Betty Lou Bender.

"Oh, look," said Bitsy, not bothering to hide the disappointment in her voice. "There's your friend, Betty Lou."

"Yeah," said Billy Joe. "She's something else. She sure can jump. Best cheerleader the school ever had."

"Well, I wouldn't know about *that*," said Bitsy.

"No, you wouldn't," agreed Billy Joe. "You've only been here a month."

"Thanks for reminding me," said Bitsy.

She noticed that Betty Lou could not take

her eyes away from the passing quarterback. Every time Beau Chapparal did his wind sprints or threw some passes downfield or just trotted by like a prize horse, Betty Lou jumped and clapped harder than ever.

"So what are you doing on this cold, windy day, sitting all by yourself in the grandstand?" asked Bitsy.

Billy Joe turned his head slightly toward her. There was definitely a devilish look in his blue eyes. "Who says I'm all alone?"

"Well," said Bitsy, "you *were* all alone until I came along."

"I like to watch the pretty girls," said Billy Joe.

It was a simple statement; an honest statement. Bitsy turned around in her seat and faced him. There was nothing cute or secretive about his remark. It was perfectly normal for a perfectly normal boy to enjoy watching perfectly normal pretty girls. Bitsy admired his forthrightness. But she had to admit she was also jealous and annoyed.

"I don't really have time for watching cheerleaders and baton twirlers," said Bitsy. "I have to go to work. But I came by to ask you a question."

"I guess you'll always be asking questions," said Billy Joe. There was no malice or nastiness in his voice. Again, he was making a simple statement. And again, Bitsy admired his honesty. But she found herself getting angry.

"I'm going to be a reporter," said Bitsy. "So it's OK to ask questions. Do you think you'd be interested in being a reporter?"

"Don't have time," Billy Joe said. "After I graduate next year, I want to join the Texas Rangers. Ever hear of them? They're like the special state police. And they need young guys who can ride horses."

"Well, I'm trying to start a student news show, a radio show," said Bitsy. "And Mr. Gonzales said if I got some student interest, he'd help with the program. Would you like to help out?"

"What would I do?" asked Billy Joe.

"I'll figure something out. So will Mr. Gonzales. You can help me. You were really good, helping me the other night."

"That was when you were scared of crickets," said Billy Joe. "I knew what to do then, but a radio show's something else. I've never done anything like that."

"You could," said Bitsy. "I mean, you could be my partner or producer. I don't care what you'd be called. We'd be a reporting . . . team. I just think it would be neat to have a five-minute show every morning. You have a nice voice. I could write the news. And you could read it. I

66

mean, with my Brooklyn accent, nobody could understand me, anyway."

"I can understand you. And I thank you for asking me. I mean that. Nobody's ever asked me to be a reporter before. Nobody's ever—"

"So can I count on you?" asked Bitsy, blushing from the sense of intimacy. "We can broadcast news about upcoming events, like rodeos. And concerts. And football games. And maybe I could do an interview. Maybe interview you?"

"On the radio?" gasped Billy Joe. "For everybody to hear. I—I'd have to think about it."

She stood up abruptly. "*Please* do, Billy Joe," said Bitsy as she gathered her schoolbooks.

She gave him one last look, and, to her delight, he gave her that beautiful smile and tipped his hat.

Chapter Seven

Bitsy was so busy concentrating on Billy Joe that Cesar Portillo had to call her name out several times before she turned around.

"Hi, Cesar," said Bitsy, as Cesar slowed down next to her in his red minibus.

A head popped up from inside the minibus. It was Tony Gomez. He looked through the window and smiled shyly.

"Can we give you a lift?" Cesar asked.

"Sure," said Bitsy. "I mean, thanks. I better get to work." She climbed into the backseat and proceeded to tell her two friends about the idea for the news program.

"Count me in," said Cesar. "Anything I can do to help, just give me a call. Maybe you can give me a title: Latino anchorman. I can translate into Spanish."

"Me, too," said Tony. "I can keep you up to date on Mexican-American events."

"I'll bet you can," said Cesar, chuckling and grinning broadly. "Like a celebration for the day the first enchilada was invented."

"Very funny," said Tony.

Bitsy sat back and tried to relax.

"OK," said Cesar. "This supersonic minibus will be cruising at ten feet, at an average of fifty-five miles per hour. Weather is going to be clear and windy. We expect to land at Park 'N Pick at approximately fifteen hundred hours."

Then Tony turned around to the backseat. His face was serious, but his eyes were sparkling.

"Refreshments will be served immediately," he announced. "Have a Dr Pepper."

He reached under the dashboard. Bitsy heard the pop as Tony opened the can of soda.

"Thanks," she said.

Just then, Billy Joe appeared. He came out of the darkness of the long entranceway, kicking pebbles out of his way. Without bothering to look up, he headed straight for his old pickup truck. Bitsy watched him as Cesar made a wide turn around the parking lot.

The beat-up truck pulled out and made a

left turn, in the opposite direction of Park 'N Pick.

"Cesar," said Bitsy impulsively, "follow that truck. Quick!"

"Si, señorita," said Cesar, warming to a new adventure.

"I know I'll be late for work," said Bitsy. "And I'll call them, first chance I get. But I have to know where Billy Joe Bridges goes in the afternoon."

The boys looked at each other and shrugged. Bitsy could hear Tony mutter "Women!" under his breath. But Cesar grinned at her.

"OK," he said. "After that truck!"

"Thanks, you guys," said Bitsy. "I really appreciate this."

"Come on, Tony," shouted Cesar. "Let's hear one of your great original songs. Bitsy, this character to my right is really a tremendous talent. He may not look it—"

"What do you mean, 'he may not look it'?" cried Tony.

"He may not look it," continued Cesar, "but the guy writes dynamite songs. Sings OK. Plays great guitar. Tony and Dave and Specs have a group. Maybe you can use them on the show."

"It's a good idea," said Bitsy, keeping her eyes straight ahead on the slowly moving truck. "But KALL is going to be strictly a news information and service show."

"Whatever you say, boss," said Cesar.

The truck pulled into a gas station. Billy Joe hopped out and walked slowly to the gas pump.

"Cesar," whispered Bitsy, "isn't that a public telephone booth on the next street? If I'm going to play detective, I'd better call my home office."

The minibus picked up speed, zooming past the gas station and stopping half a block up the street. Bitsy hopped out and raced to the phone.

"Hi, this is Bitsy White," she said into the cold mouthpiece. "Is Sue Ann there?"

It seemed to take forever for her friend to come to the phone, and all the time, Bitsy kept looking back to the station, watching as Billy Joe pumped his own gas. She felt that nobody in the world, certainly not Betty Lou Bender, could understand him or make him as happy as she could. Or was that the conceit of someone in love? Maybe she didn't understand him one bit, but for sure Bitsy knew she was in love, and she knew they had a lot in common. Here was a stranger, a cowboy from East Texas, who was an outsider trying to be on the inside. That sounded like a good description of herself. She sensed that Billy Joe was a dreamer, but ambitious . . . like herself.

"Bitsy, where are you?" The voice on the other end of the line broke into her thoughts. Sue Ann sounded concerned and wanted to know if Bitsy was all right.

"I'm fine," Bitsy assured her. "But I have some personal business. I can't talk about it now. I'll see you in about an hour. Can you tell Mr. Brown I've been delayed at school?"

"Sure thing," said Sue Ann. "It's pretty slow, anyway. Get here when you can. And tell *all!*"

Billy Joe got back into the truck. Bitsy hung up quickly and ran back to the patiently waiting Cesar and Tony. They followed at a safe distance behind the truck as it passed the sprawling campus of the state university, then the state capitol, traveled across the bridge that spanned the Colorado River and out into an area of trailer camps and dingy, one-level houses. Soon, Billy Joe's truck came to a stop in front of an old, white stucco building. The sign out front read: Johnson's Laundry and Dry Cleaning. Billy Joe made a sharp right turn into a small, crowded parking lot. He got out of the truck quickly and ran to a side door.

"I didn't know Billy Joe worked at Johnson's," exclaimed Tony. "That's a tough operation."

"Why?" asked Bitsy.

"It's kind of like a sweatshop. Out front, it's

your typical cleaning operation. But they have a factory back there. I know, because my cousin used to work there. All the cleaning and laundry are done on the premises. And the premises are pretty hot and steamy."

Five minutes later, a black Lincoln sedan pulled up to the store. Billy Joe ran out to the car. A door opened, and unseen hands gave him a huge bundle of laundry. Billy Joe ran back into the store. A minute later, he reemerged, loaded down with what appeared to be suits and trousers and dresses, all on hangers. Billy Joe hung the clothes carefully on hooks in the back of the car.

"Well," said Cesar. "That's a tough way to make a buck."

"Hard to be a rodeo star in a laundry," said Tony to no one in particular.

"Let's get out of here," said Bitsy. "Please. I have to get back to Park 'N Pick."

Bitsy was silent all the way back to work. So that was the secret of Billy Joe Bridges. No rodeos for him. They were just a cover for his hot, sweaty job.

"Nothing wrong with being a carhop in a laundry," said Bitsy, as the minibus pulled into the service area of Park 'N Pick.

"Who said anything was wrong?" asked Cesar.

"Yeah," said Bitsy. "Who said anything was wrong?" She thanked her friends again and promised they'd be hearing from her soon about KALL.

"And don't forget my boys," said Cesar. "When KALL goes country and western, they'll go country and western with you."

"You got a deal," said Bitsy, smiling.

She waved to Sue Ann, who waved back. Then she turned away and ran back to the minibus just as it was starting off.

"Hey, wait a minute, you guys!"

The minibus stopped. Bitsy jumped on the tiny running board and leaned inside the window.

"Please," she said. "Don't tell anyone about what we did. I mean, don't tell anyone where Billy Joe works. And don't tell anyone we followed him. I want to tell him myself, if I get up the nerve. I *mean*, maybe I won't tell him, but at least I understand him better now."

Tony's kind eyes assured her that Billy Joe's secret was safe. Cesar suddenly looked serious. He nodded solemnly. Bitsy reached over and kissed him on the cheek.

"That was very nice, señorita," said Cesar. "How about one for my friend?"

Tony blushed a deep red. Then Cesar grabbed him by the collar and pulled him toward Bitsy, who kissed him quickly.

"That's enough kissing for one day," said Cesar. "Get to work."

Bitsy jumped down, laughing, and waved goodbye. Then she walked over to a very curious Sue Ann Jones, who had observed the entire farewell scene.

"Two boyfriends!" exclaimed Sue Ann. "That's pretty hot stuff."

"Don't be silly."

"Well, exc-u-u-u-se me," said Sue Ann.

Work was slow that afternoon but the two hours left passed quickly. Bitsy told Sue Ann all about football practice and how Billy Joe seemed both distant and close—and how her new friends did her a great favor without asking too many embarrassing questions.

"Listen. You like this cowboy. Go after him."

"I *am* going after him," said Bitsy. "But he seems so reserved. Maybe I'm not being 'ladylike.'"

Sue Ann let out a short laugh. "I didn't know there were rules of behavior. I mean, what's 'ladylike' and what's 'gentlemanlike'?"

"Well," said Bitsy. "Maybe I should play hard to get, like the Ice Queen."

"She's not playing hard to get," said Sue Ann, "if I understand your story. She's just plain not interested. It's easy to play hard to get when you don't care. Anyway you don't have to play or act *anything*. Just talk straight to the guy. Don't you want him to talk straight to you?"

Bitsy smiled as she nodded her head. She resolved to have some serious talks. One would be with Mr. Gonzales. The other would be with Billy Joe Bridges.

Chapter Eight

Bitsy was hopelessly, miserably, desperately in love. She would go to bed thinking of Billy Joe. She would wake up thinking of Billy Joe. He was like a phantom cowboy, occasionally seen from a distance in the crowded corridors, loping along in a swirl of students. Once, after class on Thursday, she caught a glimpse of him on the street and smiled tentatively. He gave her a friendly wave and was gone.

Mr. White observed his daughter over evening meals. There had been a time when she would compliment him on his cooking. There had been a time when Bitsy would volunteer to prepare dinner herself. But now there was only silence at the table. Bitsy would pick at her food, hang around to clean up, then fall into an overstuffed chair and try to study.

"Beatrice," he said, "I think you're working yourself too hard. Cut down that car-hopping job to two hours a day. And tell them you need Saturdays off for your homework."

Bitsy looked up from her history textbook and nodded in agreement, but without enthusiasm.

"You're a young, attractive girl," said John White. "You work too hard and study too much. Try to meet some boys. Socialize. Get out more."

"Sure, Dad."

On Friday morning, Bitsy dragged herself out of bed, put on an old blue sweater, a pair of jeans, her Roulettes jacket, and walked out of the house. It was the first time in three years she hadn't bothered with breakfast.

Marcia was waiting impatiently alongside a streetlight. She kept circling the tall steel structure, looking at her wristwatch, then down the street. Finally, Bitsy came into view.

"You're seven minutes late," shouted Marcia. "Get those loafers moving."

"OK, Marcia."

Bitsy had been walking to school every morning with Marcia, discussing the problems of boys and crushes and infatuations and how-do-you-know-when-you-really-like-someone. They would wind up at their first classes of the day depressed and confused by those early morning walking-talks. Marcia resolved to change the mood.

"Bitsy, before you open your mouth, I have to have some serious words with you. You're getting sappy over that cowboy."

"Marcia, haven't you ever been in love?"

"Sure I have, but only after I got to know the boy," came the stern reply. "I never went around chasing dreams."

"You have to start somewhere," said Bitsy. "Besides, you seem to have it all worked out in your head. Get to know the boy after three dates; let him kiss you after . . . I don't know how many dates; swear undying love after fifty dates. I don't think real love has any rules like that."

Just then, Beau Chapparal drove by and offered them a lift.

"No, thanks," said Bitsy. "We like to walk. Nobody walks in this town. Walking is the best exercise a person can have."

"I think playing football is the best exercise," said Beau. "And it's the most fun."

"Girls don't play football," said Marcia.

"Says who?" shot back Bitsy. "Everybody used to say girls couldn't play basketball or tennis or baseball. Now they've got all kinds of professional teams. So watch out, Beau. One of these days, you may get tackled by a woman."

"I sincerely hope so," said Beau, chuckling

and giving them a wink. "Speaking of which, I have a ticket for you for the game, Bitsy. I can give it to you later. Or I can give it to you tonight."

"What's tonight?" asked Bitsy.

"Marcia'll tell you," said Beau. He waved and drove away so quickly that his tires shrieked.

"That boy sure makes a lot of noise," said Bitsy.

"That boy," said Marcia, "has a thing for you. And he's the most eligible, most good-looking boy at school. Don't you pass up a good catch. A Beau Chapparal doesn't come along every day."

"Thank goodness. I don't think my nerves could take it."

"Your nerves!" exclaimed Marcia. "Listen to you! He's a genuine football star. Get with it!"

"So what's this about tonight?" asked Bitsy. "What's going on tonight?"

"Every Friday night during the football season," explained Marcia, "the school has a dance in one of the gymnasiums. In fact, your friends are going to be the entertainment."

"My friends?"

"The Wing Dings," said Marcia impatiently. "Tony and Dave and Specs. Everybody goes to the dance. Unless you have a secret date. Do you have a secret date?"

"I wish." Bitsy sighed. "I wouldn't even mind having a not-so-secret date."

"Well maybe your cowboy will be at the dance," said Marcia. "Anyway, the football team will be there. You could do a lot worse than dancing with Beau Chapparal."

Bitsy considered this possibility. She also reminded herself that a news program could have announced the dance and the Wing Dings. Already, Bitsy felt a bit livelier. Nothing like a project, she thought, to take a person's mind off her social life—or the absence of one.

As they approached the school, Bitsy saw a beautiful young woman wearing a cowboy hat. She was surrounded by several members of the football team. It was Betty Lou Bender. She's all dressed up as if she were the Queen of the Rodeo, thought Bitsy. On the fringe of the group, hanging around the crowd of admirers, was Billy Joe Bridges.

"Look at him," said Marcia. "Trying to get a word in, while that stuck-up Ice Queen flashes smiles at the boys. I think he looks sort of silly."

Yeah, look at him, thought Bitsy. But he doesn't look silly. He looks almost scared.

"Hi, Billy Joe. Going to the dance tonight?" asked Bitsy. The words came out before she knew what she was saying. Marcia looked at her disapprovingly, then ran off to class.

"How are the crickets?" asked Billy Joe.

"You took away my fear," said Bitsy. "I actually like them now. I may even get one as a pet."

"Huh?"

Bitsy felt like kicking herself. What was she talking about, ranting on and on like some kind of idiot! "I guess cowboys and Texas Rangers don't dance," said Bitsy finally.

"Who says?"

"So you do!" said Bitsy. "Well, you'll have to prove it to me. Where I come from, deep in the heart of Flatbush, guys can dance up a storm."

"I can dance," said Billy Joe simply.

"So you'll be at the dance tonight?" asked Bitsy, swallowing hard and trying to appear cool and relaxed.

"Oh, sure," said Billy Joe. "I was just waiting to see if Betty Lou is going."

"Well, she's one of the cheerleaders," said Bitsy, accenting the word "one."

"She's the *head* cheerleader," said Billy Joe admiringly.

"And what are you?" blurted out Bitsy. "A rodeo star? A Texas Ranger? Or maybe just a carhop in a laundry?"

Her words cut through him like a steel-edged carving knife. Bitsy could not have hurt him more if she had slapped his face. Instantly she regretted her words. She felt small and stupid and jealous.

"I'm sorry," said Bitsy in a low voice.

Billy Joe pulled down his denim jacket and adjusted his red bandanna. His hands trembled slightly as he spoke. "I don't," he said in a tightly controlled voice, "know how you found out about that. And I don't appreciate people who pry into other people's business. However, I don't think there's anything wrong with what I do. It may not be very glamorous, and the money's not great, but it's something, and the job's giving me a whole lot of insight. Old man Johnson—he hardly pays his people anything. I mean, those poor Mexican ladies work for peanuts."

Bitsy had never heard him talk so much before. She could see he was nervous, even angry, and defensive about being "found out."

"I'm really sorry," Bitsy apologized again. "I don't know what made me say that."

There was a long, awkward pause. Bitsy stared down at the ground. What Billy Joe said made sense, Bitsy thought. He knew what he was talking about. Intelligence and sensitivity were hiding behind those denim clothes.

"I'll bet you'd make a good reporter," Bitsy said softly, looking up at him.

Billy Joe stared at her in disbelief. He was finding it hard to stay angry. He cleared his throat. "What makes you say that? That's the second time you've mentioned being a reporter. Not that you're wrong. But how come, out of all the professions you could name—how come you come up with being a reporter?"

The bell rang for the first period.

"Because of the radio news show I'm trying to start," said Bitsy, jumping at the sound of the bell. "I think you'd be good! Let's talk about it tonight. OK?"

"OK," said Billy Joe. "I'm definitely interested—you can count me in." Suddenly he became animated. "I'll blast the dome off the state capitol; expose corruption in high places; get stories that nobody else can get. Provided you really want me."

Yeah, thought Bitsy, he's scared and unsure underneath it all. That's what comes from being an outsider: accepting nothing at face value; questioning everything.

Bitsy practically flew to her chemistry class. She figured Billy Joe was kind of a dreamer but also kind of a braggart—and that was fine. A person's got to have a dream, she thought, or what's life all about?

Just as she reached the chemistry classroom, a voice behind her said, "Excuse me, Bitsy. Bitsy?"

She knew that voice and turned around

quickly. There was Billy Joe, breathing heavily as if he had been running.

"Just one quick favor," he whispered.

Maybe he wants to kiss me, thought Bitsy. Kind of strange, to get romantic at eight o'clock in the morning, especially with students filing into a chemistry class and all those funny smells coming out of test tubes. . . .

"If you see Betty Lou Bender," he said, interrupting her fantasy, "don't say anything about the laundry. I mean, you're not supposed to know about it, but since you found out, I'd just as soon you didn't tell anybody else, especially Betty Lou."

"Your secret is safe with me," promised Bitsy, turning sharply and marching into the class.

So much for dreams, she thought, I'd better get into this chemistry class. Because I sure don't seem to have the right chemistry for Billy Joe Bridges.

Chapter Nine

At least five hundred kids must have been in the gymnasium. The lights were turned down low. For every couple that was dancing, an equal number of single people were walking around, checking out the crowd, having conversations, while their eyes took in possible dance partners. The mood was soft and warm, thanks to the music of the Wing Dings. A series of spotlights illuminated the bandstand where the three musicians were serenading the San Jacinto students. Specs Glassberg was playing the electric keyboard. Dave Mills was playing the Fender bass guitar. And Tony Gomez was playing rhythm guitar and singing an old Waylon Jennings ballad. His sweet, lyrical sound filled the huge room.

At the entranceway, just inside the gymnasium, Bitsy stood talking to Marcia, who was wearing a beige crew-necked sweater and a beige-and-maroon tartan skirt. Bitsy had on a soft white blouse, opened at the collar, and a pair of very faded jeans. Her father had tried to argue against the jeans; so had Marcia. But now she had to admit the outfit was right for Bitsy, with her red hair and her fair complexion. At the last second, Bitsy had added a necklace of dark blue stones.

"I must confess," said her now admiring father, "you look good in that outfit. And you *know* New York cops never confess anything!"

Bitsy was determined to have fun, even though there was absolutely no sign of Billy Joe Bridges. "Besides, he's just a blue-denim package of headaches and heartaches," she said to Marcia. Marcia put her hand over her heart in a melodramatic gesture, and the two girls broke into peals of laughter. Just then, Beau Chapparal, dazzling in a blue sports jacket, white shirt, and navy slacks, made his way through the crowd. Without saying a word, Bitsy let herself be led out to the dance floor. The Wing Dings were playing an up-tempo, rocking number. Beau was a good dancer and very serious about *looking* good. Bitsy found herself enjoying dancing with him, in spite of herself.

The Wing Dings switched to a medium-tempo ballad, as Dave stepped forward into the spotlight, singing his down-home brand of music. Bitsy gave herself to the sound and beat, feeling the good vibrations from the dancers around her.

"Why, Beau, honey, what are y'all doing?"

The high-pitched, syrupy-sweet voice belonged to Betty Lou Bender. She was, of course, dazzling, as only a beauty queen could be—a rhapsody in pink and white. She simply pushed herself between Bitsy and Beau, shouting above the music, flashing a smile at Beau.

"I hear a certain Yankee girl is planning a radio news program. Doesn't that sound like fun? Bitsy, you can count me in. I wouldn't miss it for the world. I can give beauty hints to all the students."

"I'll bet you can, Betty Lou," said Bitsy, smiling sweetly. "Beau, can we continue this dance?"

As Beau led Bitsy toward the center of the floor, she could not resist a parting shot at the poised beauty queen, so filled with her own radiance.

"I'll be in touch," said Bitsy. "I'm sure we can find a place for you."

After the song ended, Beau steered a flushed Bitsy toward the soft-drink table. With a dramatic gesture of generosity, he treated her to a tall glass of lemonade.

After a few sips, Beau's face grew serious. "Are you really going ahead with your radio news show?" he asked.

"If I can get student support—volunteers and listeners."

"You can count on me," he said. "I'll be your sports commentator. Should be good practice for after I retire from the Dallas Cowboys and pursue a career with one of the networks. And I'll make sure the whole team listens. What the heck, I'll make sure the whole *school* listens."

Bitsy felt weak-kneed. She plopped herself down on a wooden bench. Maybe this gorgeous football player was OK after all. He might be stuck on himself, thought Bitsy, but he was an all-right guy.

"Beau, all I can say is thank you. I really appreciate your support."

"Well, now," said Beau. "I think you Yankee girls have to get to understand us Texas boys. We may be tough on the outside, but inside we're just softies."

He made a great show of presenting Bitsy with a complimentary ticket for the Saturday football game. "Right on the fifty-yard line," he announced.

Before Bitsy could thank him again, she heard the now-familiar tone of the lady in pink—Betty Lou Bender.

"Well, aren't we being nice," she purred. "Giving away valuable tickets!"

At that precise second, Bitsy saw Billy Joe enter the gymnasium. He looked absolutely huggable, even though—or maybe because—he was uncomfortable, all "spiffed up" in a white shirt, a black string tie, and a sports jacket—along with dress jeans and the same old boots. In spite of the fact that she knew Billy Joe was only there because of Betty Lou, Bitsy felt breathless when she saw him. I bet he's the one who blabbed about KALL to Betty Lou, she thought.

Bitsy could see that Billy Joe had spotted his beauty queen and was now making his way between the dancing couples. He was probably getting himself all worked up to ask Betty Lou to dance. And Beau was looking fondly at Bitsy. Bitsy found herself feeling kind of sick and dizzy. Her face was flushed. She felt she might fall. Was it the lemonade? Was it Beau's after-shave lotion? Was it the blue-eyed boy with the big smile—for Betty Lou?

"Hi, everybody," announced Billy Joe.

"I think I'm getting sick," said Bitsy faintly.

"Billy Joe," said the Ice Queen, "why don't you take this girl home before she becomes violently ill? And, Beau, don't you open your mouth to volunteer. You owe me a dance. You promised me at school yesterday. Remember?"

"Yeah, I remember," said Beau, "and I'm a

90

man of my word." But he looked at Bitsy like a lovesick calf.

Bitsy smiled up at him, as much a smile of relief as anything else. "I'll be OK," she said. "Go on. Enjoy yourselves."

Billy Joe had said hello to Bitsy, but his eyes were still on Betty Lou. This was more than Bitsy could take. She sniffed back a tear and turned on her heels. Without saying goodbye to Marcia, Bitsy ran out of the gymnasium. As soon as she got outside, she felt better. She began the long walk back up the hill, shivering in the unexpected chill of autumn.

All Texas boys were strange to Bitsy. Even a big guy like Beau could be led around by the nose by a self-centered beauty queen. But she *was* grateful to Beau for offering to help—along with Cesar and the others—to get KALL off the ground.

"May as well celebrate KALL," she said to herself. "Nothing else seems to be working out." Shaking her head sadly, she continued her walk home.

Chapter Ten

On Monday, Bitsy presented Mr. Gonzales with the results of her week-long efforts on behalf of KALL. Beau would cover sports. Cesar would cover Hispanic events. Betty Lou would specialize in social events. Each of the Wing Dings would contribute to news of musical events. Marcia would keep abreast of cultural activities. And Bitsy would be the executive producer and chief reporter. She had prepared a petition collecting signatures in support of KALL. Thanks to Beau and the San Jacinto Steers, the weekend had produced over three hundred signatures. The communications instructor was impressed. He ordered a staff meeting for two o'clock on Wednesday afternoon.

By Tuesday afternoon, rumors of the radio show had spread through the corridors of the school like a sagebrush fire. Bitsy could not suppress her excitement. Her project was actually going to get off the ground! Nevertheless, she tried to talk sensibly to herself, listening to the voice of reason within her advising her to remain calm and not to get carried away.

You got carried away by a cowboy on a horse, whispered the voice, and all you got was a broken heart.

Now another voice interrupted Bitsy's thoughts as she hurried to her English class. The voice had a smooth, rich sound, clear and strong yet effortless. Bitsy turned around and saw the beautiful Elizabeth Ho.

"You're Bitsy White, aren't you?" she asked.

"And you're Elizabeth Ho. Nice to meet you."

"I've seen you at lunchtime," said Elizabeth. "You're always hanging out at the music table."

"With the Wing Dings," said Bitsy, feeling good about her new friends. Elizabeth chatted on about Specs and Dave and about how much she and her family enjoyed their new home in Texas, though she felt a little homesick for Viet Nam.

"Yeah," admitted Bitsy. "Much as I got to hate it there, sometimes I feel a little homesick for Brooklyn. Maybe someday I'll go back. I don't know. How about you?"

"Someday." Elizabeth sighed. "Maybe. But there's so much to do and learn every day that I don't usually get a chance to feel homesick. Texas is quite a place, isn't it?"

The girls laughed, sharing the same response—an overwhelming sense of awe at the vastness of the land and the uniqueness of the people.

"Bitsy," said Elizabeth finally, "I heard from Specs and Dave about your radio show. I'd love to be involved. I'll do anything."

"I have an idea," said Bitsy, measuring her words carefully. "Your voice. . . ." Bitsy's idea was rapidly forming. "Your voice is just as beautiful as you are, Elizabeth."

Elizabeth blushed.

"It's true," continued Bitsy. "You have a terrific voice. I think you should be the voice of KALL. How about it?"

Elizabeth's eyes opened wide. For a fleeting second, she seemed about to say no. But then she nodded once, slowly, then several times, quickly. "You've got yourself a deal," said Elizabeth.

After school, Bitsy walked slowly in the direction of Park 'N Pick. She realized she was no longer upset about Billy Joe Bridges. Everything was going so well, she just couldn't stay upset for long. Maybe Billy Joe was just a scared kid from a small town, trying to come on strong, bragging about rodeos and Texas Rangers and running after beauty queens but really feeling insecure and shy. And suddenly there he was, sitting in the back of his pickup truck, his legs dangling over the side. Bitsy's heart started to pound. Now that he was actually right there, she couldn't think so coolly. As she approached him, he actually tipped his big hat to her. Bitsy was delighted.

"How are you feeling?" he asked, his blue eyes warm with concern. "I mean, after the dance. I went looking for you to give you a ride home, but you just disappeared. I got a little worried."

"I'm feeling much better, thank you."

She tried to read his blue eyes, tried to figure out what was really going on inside him. Billy Joe seemed to come by his friendly way quite naturally. His voice was musical. His blue eyes twinkled. He seemed more at ease today.

"Heard lots of talk about your radio show," he said. "Even signed one of those petitions."

"Thank you," said Bitsy softly. To herself she said, Radio show—think radio show—don't think of him.

"I've got an idea for a special news story," he said. "If you're interested in hearing about it."

"Sure."

"Can I drive you to work?"

She shrugged her shoulders, trying to appear indifferent. There was just so much rejection a person could take. She wanted to stay cool, wanted to use her head instead of her heart. If he wanted to make a fool of himself over Betty Lou, she, Bitsy, was going to get hurt, unless she played it smart. So Bitsy swore up and down and sideways she would *not* make a fool of herself over this cowboy. But she knew her heart wasn't listening to a word.

Billy Joe hopped down off the truck, landing lightly on the sidewalk. He opened the door and extended a hand to Bitsy, guiding her into the front seat. As Billy Joe slammed the door shut and ran to the driver's side, Bitsy felt that special thrill. His touch had done it. His hand was gentle, yet strong. He behaved like a gentleman of the world, while the boy inside was shy. Surely Billy Joe Bridges was a maze of contradictions. And wasn't Bitsy White a maze— a mess—of contradictions, too? In spite of all her resolve, she felt tremors at the prospect of being alone with him in the front seat of his truck.

For a few minutes, he drove in silence. His normally clear forehead had two deep worry lines. His eyes seemed to be somewhere else, not on the road. Finally he spoke.

"I have an idea for a story," he announced.

"I don't know if I can write it by myself, but maybe I can just mosey around getting facts. Maybe we could do it together."

Bitsy was certain he could hear her heavily pounding heart. Of course, they· could do it together. Billy Joe could drive to Alaska for all Bitsy cared—as long as they could do it together. Her heart was saying yes, yes, a thousand times yes, while her head fought to stay cool.

"I'm listening," she said finally, not daring to look at him.

"Dry cleaning!" he announced, with a wave of his right hand.

"What?"

"Dry cleaning," he repeated.

"What about dry cleaning?"

"Well, not just dry cleaning. Laundry, too," he added.

"I'm all ears," said Bitsy, getting slightly alarmed. What on earth was he talking about?

"It's like this. . . ." said Billy Joe in a shaky voice.

Then Bitsy realized Billy Joe was very nervous. "Take your time," said Bitsy. "I don't care if I'm a few minutes late for work. I really want to hear what you've got to say." In her effort to relax him, Bitsy was able to relax herself. She smiled warmly at Billy Joe, and leaned against the door so she faced him.

"Well," he began, "old man Johnson, who

runs the place I'm working at, is getting a lot of cheap labor from south of the border. He's paying slave wages to these Mexican women because they're so hungry to get any kind of money for their families. But it also means the folks around here—the natives—can't get any jobs for themselves. They're not going to work for slave wages. They're poor. But they've got pride."

Bitsy breathed a sigh of relief. She liked the story idea. She also felt a great surge of sympathy for Billy Joe. His boss, this "old man Johnson," was probably also paying "slave wages" to *him*. And Billy Joe had to swallow his pride, precisely because he was poor.

"Now, Bitsy, you have to promise me my name won't get mentioned in all of this. I can't afford to lose my job, even if it's only part-time and even if it's only temporary."

"I understand," said Bitsy. And she did.

"So what do you think of my—idea?"

Bitsy wanted to hug him. "It's an excellent idea," said Bitsy. "Come to the staff meeting at Gonzales's office—that's the Communications Department. It's Wednesday afternoon at two o'clock. Your story—"

"Our story," he corrected her.

"Our story will be the first feature story for KALL. We can call it . . . 'Dirty Laundry.' "

Billy Joe laughed nervously. The truck pulled into the Park 'N Pick driving lot.

"Now I can't stay long at the meeting," cautioned Billy Joe. "I do have a job."

"I'll make sure it's the first item on the agenda," said Bitsy. "Well, Billy Joe, I'll see you Wednesday afternoon."

No sooner had she gotten out of the truck, feeling hopelessly in love but hopeful about the story, than a sparkling white Chevette screeched to a halt beside her. It was Beau Chapparal. Again.

"How are you feeling?" he asked. "Sorry I missed you."

So here was Bitsy White, between two boys. Her secret love was up there in the truck, nervous about his news story. And her open admirer, smelling of after-shave lotion, was ready to follow her to the ends of the earth—provided he didn't get tackled by Betty Lou.

"Hot news item for KALL," announced Beau Chapparal. "The school is having its first fall picnic in two weeks; Sunday after next. How about it? Will you go with me?"

Bitsy leaned against the truck. She counted to ten, hoping against hope that Billy Joe would match the offer.

"I don't know, Beau."

"It's going to be right on the shores of Lake Austin," said Beau. "Real pretty."

"That's right," chimed in Billy Joe. "Real pretty."

"Hey, Billy Joe," said Beau. "I'll bet a certain gorgeous cheerleader with the initials B.L.B. wouldn't mind being asked."

"Well, I don't know about that," said Billy Joe. "But thanks for the advice."

That did it, thought Bitsy. "Beau," she said, in a voice that carried well into the cabin of the old pickup truck, "you got yourself a date for that picnic."

"Eeeeeeyahoooo," shouted Beau, in his best Texas drawl.

"And don't either of you boys forget the meeting on Wednesday afternoon."

She turned away and marched toward the greasy smell of chiliburgers. Boys, she thought. I've had enough of them. Enough of cowboys, anyway!

Chapter Eleven

When the KALL staff finally settled down on Wednesday afternoon, when the nervous murmurings and the whispers and the buzzing tuned all the way down to a tense silence, Mr. Gonzales cleared his throat and addressed the students.

"I've got good news for everybody," he said. "Frankly, I can't believe how cooperative people are. Mr. McCoy, our school superintendent, has already put up loudspeakers and wiring connecting the third-floor studio with the cafeteria. Also, our local radio station is making Sunday night available—from six to six-fifteen—so we can do our special stories as well as our listing of special events."

There was a scattering of applause from the group.

"Bitsy has come up with a lot of talented youngsters," he continued. "I'm pleased that Betty Lou Bender and Elizabeth Ho and Beau Chapparal and Cesar Portillo and—"

Mr. Gonzales paused to take a long look at the three-by-five index card he had cupped in his hand. Then he put on his reading glasses to check something.

"The Wing Dings," supplied Dave.

"The Wing Dings?" inquired Mr. Gonzales. "Is that really the name of your group?"

"Pretty neat, huh?" said Dave proudly.

"I don't know if it's neat," said Mr. Gonzales, "but it *is* colorful. Anyway, I want to welcome all of you to KALL, and I want to thank Bitsy White for putting it all together."

Again there was a burst of applause. Betty Lou Bender, however, refrained from clapping. She was concentrating her charms on Beau. Not that the rest of the group was all that wrapped up in the little lecture Mr. Gonzales was delivering. As the teacher went on talking about responsibility and professionalism and meeting deadlines and school spirit, Bitsy noticed lots of interplay. Cesar Portillo, his blue-black hair gleaming, kept his flashing eyes on the beautiful Elizabeth Ho. While Cesar appeared to be listening to the communications teacher, he was noticing every move or murmur from the girl on his left. Betty Lou was giving off great waves of charm and sociability to Beau, acting as if she were the hostess of the occasion. And then the door opened suddenly and in walked Billy Joe. He nodded shyly to Mr. Gonzales, then to Bitsy and made a beeline for the Ice Queen. He sat down directly in front of her, then turned sideways in his seat, his long legs out in the aisle, so that he could see both Mr. Gonzales and Betty Lou. Only Elizabeth Ho was fully attentive to Mr. Gonzales's speech.

What a crew! thought Bitsy. It's going to be a miracle if any work gets done. Mr. Gonzales handed out the assignments, made arrangements for the next meeting, and wished everyone good luck. Cesar stood up, brushed some imaginary dust from his leather jacket, held the door open for Elizabeth, and followed her out into the hallway. Beau started to say something to Bitsy but was quickly grabbed by Betty Lou and pulled outside. Bitsy had to marvel at her. No redhead from Brooklyn, New York, was going to stand in the way of Betty Lou.

I wonder, thought Bitsy, if I could just grab Billy Joe and drag him away? Maybe I can look him squarely in his eyes, his blue, blue eyes, and pin him down for a date? Maybe we could go canoeing on Lake Austin? Maybe I should ask *him* to the picnic? Maybe—

Good grief, she mused, no wonder they call me the Question-Mark Kid. Lots of questions; no answers.

When she came out of her reverie, Bitsy discovered she was sitting by herself in an empty classroom. The meeting had broken up. She heaved a sigh and headed for her locker.

The rest of the day dragged on and on. Her job at Park 'N Pick seemed never-ending. Sue Ann and Bitsy were too busy to talk, but Sue Ann already knew the reason for Bitsy's tight-lipped expression. Finally it was six o'clock, and Bitsy went to change back into her street clothes.

"Hey," said Sue Ann, "lose that long face. You're a big star. You've got your own radio show. And the word is out that you and Billy Joe are into 'Dirty Laundry.' "

Sue Ann laughed at her little joke. Bitsy shot her a look that wiped out the laughter.

"Sue Ann, I'm so miserable. Life has lost its meaning." Even Bitsy couldn't suppress a giggle at those words. Her laughter broke the ice. But a few giggles couldn't relieve the melancholy mood.

"Beatrice, I can't stand to see you so terrible," said Sue Ann. "There's no reason in the world why you have to be worrying and fretting over some boy. I keep telling you to take the bull by the horns."

"What do you mean?"

"If you step outside, I'll show you," said Sue Ann.

They walked out the door and into the October dusk. A slight breeze was in the air, a welcome coolness after three hours of car-hopping. Sue Ann pointed a finger at a crazy old hulk of a car. It was a chrome-plated, four-door Oldsmobile, covered with a fresh coat of yellow paint.

"Isn't she gorgeous?" Sue Ann sighed. "I just bought her yesterday. Isn't she the most sensational old wreck of a gas-guzzling car you ever laid eyes on?"

"Well," said Bitsy, slowly, "it does have four wheels. It's—ummm—it's unusual."

"Unusual?" cried Sue Ann. "It's downright strange! I mean, isn't this the most bizarre car you've ever seen? But I tell you, she's an attention-getter. I mean, several boys pulled up this afternoon asking me all kinds of questions. About the car, that is. But you understand that this car is a reflection of *me*. Some of those fellows were probably wondering what kind of young lady drives around in this old wreck. I tell you, Bitsy, my phone's going to be ringing."

"I'm very happy for you," said Bitsy. "But what's that got to do with me? What's that got to do with taking the bull by the horns? Should I get a car like this and park it outside the school?"

"You could do a lot worse, honey," said Sue Ann. "But my plan is for you and me to go for a little spin. Right *now*. Tell your daddy you'll be a few minutes late for dinner."

"I get it!" cried Bitsy. "Then you and I head over to Johnson's Laundry."

"You have to talk to the boy anyway, don't you?"

"Absolutely," said Bitsy, feeling the blood rush through her body as her heart pumped madly. "It's about time we got started on our special assignment."

Fifteen minutes later, the Oldsmobile was sputtering across the bridge to the poor part of town. As they pulled into the laundry parking area, Bitsy suddenly grabbed Sue Ann's arm. "That's Billy Joe's truck coming toward us. Turn around —follow him. Quick!"

Billy Joe drove by without seeing them. Sue Ann let out a groan and turned the car around. They followed the pickup truck for several miles, further and further away from the bridge. Now they were practically at the city limits. The highway to San Antonio stretched ahead of them. Billy Joe turned off the main road, weaving the truck through winding streets. Drab, tiny wooden houses were all around them. Then Billy Joe turned into a dead-end. At the end of the unpaved road was a rusty trailer. Behind the trailer, Bitsy could make out a falling-down barn. Between the barn and the trailer was a fenced-in patch of land, which Sue Ann identified as a corral. Billy Joe's horse was standing there, like a statue, staring at the approaching vehicles.

Sue Ann pulled up behind the truck.

"Billy Joe," shouted Bitsy, "wait up a second. I have to talk to you."

The cowboy's mouth fell open. He stared at the old car, then blinked his eyes and gulped hard when he saw the two young women. Sue Ann waved from behind the wheel. Bitsy jumped out and ran over to him.

"Were you following me?" he asked finally, through clenched teeth.

"Please don't be mad," said Bitsy. "You don't have a phone. At least I couldn't find any Bridges in the book. And you have a way of disappearing right after class. We have to discuss our assignment," she rushed on. "Sue Ann and I got to the laundry just as you were leaving. So we had to follow you. Can we talk?"

"Well," said Billy Joe, "the trailer's kind of a

mess. And I haven't had a chance to put anything down on paper, and. . . ." He went on to
explain that it was his responsibility to prepare
dinner for his mother and his kid brother. His
mother worked all day in a factory. She would
pick up little Willie at the day-care center, and
they'd be getting back in about an hour.

"That's OK," said Bitsy. "I've got my cas-
sette. I can do an interview with you, ask you
all these questions I've prepared, and later put
everything down on paper. I'll just ask the questions. You supply the answers. We can sit outside if you want to."

Billy Joe looked very relieved at this sug-
gestion.

So for the next forty minutes, while Sue
Ann fed the horse and hung around the make-
shift corral, Bitsy and Billy Joe sat outside the
narrow trailer, recording the questions and answers that would eventually make up the news
special.

When it was finally time for Bitsy to leave,
Billy Joe ran over to the car to say goodbye.
"Bitsy," he said, "I want you to know this is the
most important thing I've ever done. I really feel
good. I feel like I accomplished something
important."

He held out his large hand, and Bitsy
reached out. They shook hands solemnly, as if

a big deal had just been closed. And as the Oldsmobile huffed and puffed its way out of the dead-end, Sue Ann talking on and on about old cars and old horses, Bitsy White knew, as she'd never known before, that Billy Joe Bridges was indeed . . . a big deal.

Chapter Twelve

A special KALL meeting was held the next afternoon. Robert Gonzales puffed nervously on his dark pipe, flashing a quick smile as Bitsy and Marcia flopped down in the front row. Billy Joe trudged in, looking worn out. He sat in the back row, near the door, but his attention was on Mr. Gonzales. Bitsy turned around and waved at him in a friendly greeting, but the cowboy only returned her gesture with a tight-lipped grin. Specs, Dave, and Tony entered noisily, carrying their guitar cases. They took seats next to the window and placed their cases carefully against the wall. Beau came in next, with his orange duffel bag over his shoulder, and stood inside the door, trying to decide on the best seat. Betty Lou, Elizabeth, and Cesar were in the center of the room talking quietly. Beau sat down behind Betty Lou and put his bag down heavily.

"Hi, Beau," said Betty Lou, flashing her most winning smile.

"Everybody here?" asked Mr. Gonzales. He nodded to each of the students, smiling at them.

"OK," he said. "I just want to congratulate each of you on the job you're doing. The response from faculty and students alike—not to mention the community—has been excellent."

He continued praising them, but Bitsy impatiently drummed her fingers. Come on, let's get on with it, she thought.

"And now," went on Mr. Gonzales, "I want to talk to you about the project Bitsy and Billy Joe have suggested. Good idea. Great idea. But— it's too risky. I've already gotten some negative reactions from our principal and from . . . a few other people."

Who were the "few other people"? Bitsy wondered.

"The problem is," said Gonzales, "we'd have some high-school kids going on the air, accusing a respectable businessman of importing cheap labor."

"Slave labor," interrupted Bitsy.

Billy Joe fidgeted in his seat, waiting for everyone to turn around and stare at him. But

111

all eyes were riveted on the perspiring, pipe-smoking teacher.

"Now, the school could get sued," continued Mr. Gonzales. "We got permission to have a student news show partly because it was supposed to be safe—free of controversial subjects. You see, the main purpose of KALL—and I'm sure Bitsy would agree with me—is to teach all of you how to run a radio program. . . ."

"And to perform a service to the community," insisted Bitsy, who could barely contain her anger and impatience.

Mr. Gonzales looked down at her. Now there was genuine sympathy in his eyes. "I'm sorry," he said.

"Don't apologize to me," said Bitsy. "Apologize to Billy Joe. He put a lot of work into the project."

Bitsy turned around and looked directly into Billy Joe's eyes. He met her look. This time, though, he did not turn away.

"Well, I don't see what all the fuss is about," cried Betty Lou. "It's just a bunch of people working in a laundry. Heck, they should be happy they've got jobs."

"They're being exploited," said Billy Joe suddenly, "because they're poor and ignorant. They don't know any better." For the first time, Billy Joe stopped looking at Betty Lou as if he were a lovesick puppy.

"Hey," shouted Tony, "I had relatives working there. Are you calling them stupid?" The usually mild-mannered Tony was furious.

"Tony," said Billy Joe, "I work in that laundry. Because I'm poor and I don't have a choice. That's why."

Betty Lou turned around and began laughing at Billy Joe, shaking her head all the while. "Now I thought you were a big-time rodeo star, Billy Joe. Shame on you."

Bitsy sprang up out of her seat like a jack-in-the-box. She marched down the aisle and faced the blond beauty.

"Bitsy—" began Mr. Gonzales. "Get back in your seat."

"Betty Lou Bender," cried Bitsy, ignoring the teacher, "if you don't apologize to Billy Joe, I'm going to give you a present straight out of Flatbush. We call it a fist sandwich. Now apologize." The Ice Queen looked first to Mr. Gonzales, then to Beau. Finally, Bitsy returned to her seat.

"Betty Lou," said Mr. Gonzales, "you do owe Billy Joe an apology."

"Well, all right then," snapped Betty Lou. "I apologize."

She headed for the door. When she put her hand on the knob, she turned quickly to Beau, who was looking nervously from her to Bitsy.

"You coming, Beau?" asked the beauty queen.

"I'll see you at the field," he said, like a conspirator. "Honest!" And then Betty Lou was gone.

Mr. Gonzales took off his tweed jacket and dropped it absentmindedly across the desk.

"I'm afraid it's all my fault," he confessed. "I've got this reputation for being a popular teacher, but that's because I've always played it safe. A show like 'Dirty Laundry' would get some powerful people angry."

His voice dropped, and everyone in the room, including Bitsy and Marcia in the front row, had to lean forward to hear him.

"And," he continued, "I'm afraid I could lose my job. You see, Billy Joe? I'm in the same position you're in. Only you're willing to do something about it. And I'm chicken."

Then Mr. Gonzales left the room. A moment later, while everyone sat there in stunned silence, he returned, scooped up his jacket, and vanished. A cloud of pipe smoke trailed behind him.

Bitsy stood up, turned around, and faced the group. "Well?" she asked. "What now?"

Billy Joe remained seated, staring straight ahead at the clean blackboard. He looked, thought Bitsy, as if he had just been thrown from a horse. She walked up the aisle and stood alongside him. Then she nudged him gently on his arm. He acknowledged her touch, then shrugged his shoulders in a gesture of helplessness. At that moment they could have been alone in the classroom. No one existed except the two of them. Bitsy knew their hard-hitting exposé was not a failure. Billy Joe had exposed himself, revealed the truth of his own poverty. His fantasy world was crumbling: the Ice Queen had scorned him, and the image of himself as rodeo star was shattered. But he was finally opening his eyes—and Bitsy was there, standing beside him.

As the kids straggled out to the parking lot after the meeting, Billy Joe turned to Bitsy. "Hey, it's OK," he said. "There'll be other stories to report." He touched her arm and Bitsy's heart soared. "C'mon," said Billy Joe. "I've got my horse. I'll give you a ride to work."

"Hey, Muffin," shouted Billy Joe to the old brown-and-white mare, "I want you to meet my new friend. Now you take good care of her."

Bitsy decided to be totally honest. As she approached Muffin, Bitsy clutched at Billy Joe's sleeve.

"Hey, Bitsy, you're squeezing the blood out of my arm."

"I'm scared," confessed Bitsy. "That animal is huge. I don't know if I should trust her. I mean, I always wanted to ride. And I particularly wanted to ride your horse, ever since that first morning I saw you, but. . . ."

"Well, then," said Billy Joe, "no sweat. You just get right up there. It's easy, and Muffin is gentle as a lamb."

He helped Bitsy put her left foot in the stirrup, then stepped back as she swung onto the horse. Bitsy leaned forward as Billy Joe untied the reins from the parking meter and handed them to her.

"Sit up straight," he said. "Keep your weight balanced, as if you had a pole straight up your spine. And don't worry about your arms. She'll respond to your thighs and calves."

Bitsy took a deep breath and tried to walk Muffin around the parking lot. Specs, Tony, Dave, Cesar, and Elizabeth Ho were now crossing the parking lot toward Billy Joe. They all had big smiles on their faces. And Marcia Mobley was running behind Bitsy, laughing hysterically.

"Are we doing a new program," she cried out, "on Rider Education?"

"I think we should do a show called 'Horse Abuse,' " shouted Cesar.

"You guys stop kidding around," cried Bitsy. Suddenly Billy Joe took a deep breath and hoisted himself up onto the horse. Bitsy was stunned. She had to remind herself to sit up straight. She really wanted to lean back and lose herself in Billy Joe's warm flannel shirt and denim jacket. His arms felt strong and secure around her. She could feel his heartbeat. Meanwhile, the rest of the kids watched the spectacle and talked among themselves about the radio show. Tony strummed his guitar softly. Suddenly he came down hard on his guitar, causing everyone to look up.

"I got it. I have the next story for our show. Do you remember," he said, "the band that played out at that rowdy nightclub called the Chicken Coop last year? It was Friday Night Amateur Hour when almost anyone can play. And even with chicken wire across the stage for protection, two of the band members got hurt when people in the audience started throwing bottles. The Chicken Coop is a public menace."

Bitsy grabbed Billy Joe's hand. "That could be our story," she whispered.

She looked down at Tony and smiled. "Thank you," she said. "You've come up with a great idea. We'll—we'll pose as a group and perform at the Chicken Coop and write up a firsthand account of what goes on out there. Ahem! Bitsy and the Wing Dings. That's going to be the special name of this special group. Besides, you fellows need a female voice." Marcia and Elizabeth looked up with interest.

"I like it already," said Specs. "We need some new blood in our band."

"Don't like it too much," warned Bitsy. "I'm

only coming out of retirement for the sake of the story. Billy Joe could come to the club, hiding a little tape recorder in a bag. I'll start singing, with you boys backing me up. We'll get Beau Chapparal there as a decoy. He'll tape us out in the open. When the management objects, the crowd is sure to start trouble. Sounds like that kind of crowd will look for any excuse to riot. And we'll have our story."

"That was my idea," said Tony, to anyone who would listen. "Hey, Cesar, you hear that?"

Billy Joe just sat quietly, keeping Muffin calm. But he was becoming aware of the girl sharing his saddle. Her hair had a smell of wild flowers. Betty Lou could go on twirling her batons. Here was a real, intelligent, caring, good-looking girl—literally under his nose.

"I better get you to work," he said. "But you can count me in. I mean, with your Chicken Coop story."

The three Wing Dings were huddled by the back of the minibus, arguing over this sudden turn in their careers. Finally, there was silence.

"My buddies and I," began Dave, "are willing to go along with the program. We just want to warn you that there's going to be a whole mess of rehearsals. And if we're going to do it, it better be soon. Like in a couple of weeks."

"It's a deal," shouted Bitsy.

"Let's go, Muffin," shouted Billy Joe. "Giddap."

There was only the hollow sound of the mare's hooves on the asphalt. Bitsy was strongly aware of the powerful animal beneath her. Now she had everything to look forward to—Billy Joe, the Wing Dings, the danger of the Chicken Coop, the excitement of a big news story. And when Billy Joe finally brought Muffin to a halt in front of Park 'N Pick, Sue Ann Jones saw a huge, wonderful smile on Bitsy's face.

Chapter Thirteen

On Saturday afternoon Dave drove his motorcycle into Park 'N Pick. His news almost made Bitsy drop a big tray of tamaleburgers.

"The only time I could get for the Chicken Coop," he said, "is next Friday night. That gives us six days to rehearse. Think you can handle three original songs?"

"Sure," said Bitsy. "It just means I have to give up my social life." She laughed grimly to herself. The closest thing she'd had to a social life was sitting on a horse with Billy Joe Bridges. He hadn't made another move toward her since then.

"We're going to rehearse tonight. I'll pick you up at seven o'clock," said Dave.

"Great," said Bitsy. "See you then."

As he roared out of the parking lot, Marcia Mobley and her mother drove up alongside the dazed carhop.

"Hey, Bitsy," shouted Marcia, bringing her out of her reverie. "Where have you been hiding? I'll bet that cowboy is taking up all your time."

Bitsy just smiled mysteriously and let it pass.

No sooner had she taken the Mobleys' lunch order than Beau Chapparal drove up in his shining white convertible.

"Bitsy," he shouted, "I have to talk to you. It's important." Marcia and her mother watched all this in total fascination. They strained, unsuccessfully, to catch the whispered words.

"Good luck today," said Bitsy. "Hit a home run for me."

"This is football, not baseball," said Beau disgustedly.

"Oh, I'm sorry. It's just that I'm busy," said Bitsy. "See all these cars waiting to be served?"

"Well," said Beau, "I just had to tell you I can't take you to that picnic. Coach wants me to rest up for the big game."

Bitsy looked right through the weakly smiling athlete. His anxious eyes gave him away.

"Who's your coach?" said Bitsy. "Betty Lou Bender?"

121

She turned and flounced into the kitchen. Beau had probably seen the light at last: Bitsy was just too independent, too involved in other things for him. In her heart of hearts, Bitsy was relieved. If she went to the big picnic with anyone, she still hoped and prayed it would be Billy Joe. Now the way was clear for the cowboy to step in and ask her out. Oh, yes, she thought, the way is clear—only Billy Joe doesn't know the way.

"What are you mumbling about?" asked Sue Ann. "And don't tell me. I know. But I have to warn you, you're spreading yourself pretty thin."

Bitsy knew her friend was right. She also knew things were coming to a head. She couldn't go on this way—working and studying and doing the radio show, not to mention her combination debut-and-farewell appearance with the Wing Dings! And over everything loomed the tall shadow of Billy Joe Bridges.

Chapter Fourteen

Thursday night was the final rehearsal. At six o'clock, Bitsy was working her way through the huge tuna fish salad her father had painstakingly prepared. She knew she had to eat something to keep up her strength. She also knew her father had always boasted that she was a "good eater." But this particular salad seemed to be in a bottomless bowl. Besides, her feet ached from car-hopping. Her voice felt strained from nervousness as well as rehearsals. And the student news show, even though it was only five minutes every day, did require preparation. Bitsy just wanted to rest her head and dream of Billy Joe lifting her onto his stallion and riding off into a red sunset. An insistent honking suddenly roused her—while it provoked her quick-tempered father.

"Tell your friend to come inside," he grumbled. "Sounds like a lovesick goose."

"No, I better just get going," said Bitsy.

Five minutes later, she was kissing her dad good night. She ran out the door and jumped into Dave's yellow sports car. The drive along Red River was breathtaking, and Bitsy was almost sorry when they pulled into the driveway of the Gomez home. Nerves, she told herself, as she and Dave joined the others in the living room.

The first number was an original that Specs had written. It was called "Cotton Candy Cutey," an up-tempo song that required more of a sense of rhythm than an experienced sound. Bitsy had a naturally sweet voice, and when she sang with the Wing Dings, her responsibility to the boys was so strong she concentrated fully on all three guitars. Her voice became another instrument.

When the song ended, Bitsy was startled to hear the sound of applause. It came from the kitchen. Mama and Papa Gomez and Tony's three older sisters and two older brothers were sitting over sliced oranges, enjoying the live music from the living room. For just an instant, Bitsy yearned for her own mother, but she quickly shut the thought away.

"Hey," cried Bitsy, grinning. "How about that?"

"Don't get carried away," said Specs. "Your voice sounds a little tight. I think we have a lot of work to do."

Bitsy took a deep breath and looked out the window. There was a thin sliver of a moon, razor sharp in the starry sky. It looked like a nice night for a ride—on a horse or in a pickup truck.

While Specs worked out the harmonics and the changes, Bitsy continued to stare out into the cool autumn evening. Dave and Tony were arguing about something technical that Bitsy didn't understand. But she had faith in the three young men.

She wished she had the same faith in Billy Joe. Where was he tonight? Bitsy wondered. Sitting in that cramped, narrow trailer, trying to study? Or could he possibly be thinking of her? Bitsy looked at her reflection in the window and made a face. Aside from a few freckles, she wasn't bad looking. Kind of cute, she thought. Interesting looking. Now she pressed her upturned nose against the cold windowpane. Beyond the barren front yard, the street was deserted. But she continued to look, wildly hoping that Billy Joe Bridges would magically appear and wait for her by the wooden gate.

Her thoughts were interrupted by the plunk-

ing of a guitar and the tenor voice of Specs
Glassberg.

" 'Cotton Candy Cutey.' One more time."

It would not be "one more time." It would
be many more times—until they got it right. It
would be a long evening.

The rehearsal finally broke up at midnight.
Bitsy could just picture her father sitting up in
bed, reading a mystery novel and peering over
his reading glasses at the clock-radio.

"Tony, can I use your phone? I think my
dad's going to kill me." Bitsy did a quick prayer
as she dialed the number. One ring later, the
clear, strong voice of her father came through,
with the simple command that his daughter be
home in fifteen minutes or there would be no
musical debut.

When Bitsy hung up the phone, she saw
that Tony had his San Jacinto sweatshirt on.

"I'm driving you home," said Tony. "Dave'll
take Specs home."

"That was a good rehearsal," Dave said. "I
think we're ready for the Chicken Coop."

"But is the Chicken Coop ready for us?"
asked Bitsy. "I'm scared."

"Bitsy," said Specs, "you did fine. You know
the songs. You know the arrangements. Now go
home and get a good night's sleep."

Specs and Dave waved good night as Bitsy

suspiciously eyed Tony's beat-up car. "Are you sure you can drive it?"

Tony nodded. "Don't worry. I've driven this thing before."

"This thing" managed to wheeze its way past two traffic lights. Then it quietly died. Bitsy and Tony had to push it to a curb. Meanwhile, Bitsy was getting more frightened by the second. Where were they? Somewhere in the old Mexican quarter, somewhere across the bridge. And then a thought struck Bitsy. The bridge! Billy Joe! The trailer! The dead-end!

"Yeah," confirmed Tony. "I know Billy Joe's trailer. It's up that street, then up a hill, then over to a dead-end. But I'm sure he's asleep!"

Billy Joe *was* asleep. So was his mother, his kid brother, and the old horse in the barn. But by the time Bitsy called out his name half a dozen times, she succeeded in waking up the entire Bridges family—including Muffin. Billy Joe stuck his sleepy head out the door. Bitsy thought he looked cute in his long johns and his bare feet. When Billy Joe saw her, he ducked back inside; then reemerged moments later in his jeans and denim jacket.

"I feel awful having to do this," said Bitsy. "But Tony was driving me home and his car broke down."

"Say no more," said Billy Joe graciously. "I'll get you both home."

"Billy Joe? Who's out there?"

"Friends, Ma," he called back, winking at Bitsy. He ran inside to explain things to his mother and was back in two minutes. "Let's go!"

Bitsy and Tony piled into the cabin of the truck alongside Billy Joe. Roaring out of the dead-end and flying across the bridge, the truck pulled up alongside the Gomez home in three and a half minutes. Tony jumped out and waved good night.

"You drive like a madman," Bitsy said as Billy Joe sped down the road. But her big eyes were ablaze with admiration and excitement. The look was not lost on Billy Joe.

"Yeah," said Billy Joe. "But I'm good."

He did, however, slow down considerably on the way back. The streetlights revealed peaceful, gently winding streets that were free of crickets. Bitsy stretched out her legs in the spacious cabin.

Neither of them spoke. But Bitsy felt very comfortable on the way home. Home! This was her new home; her new neighborhood; her new community. And maybe Billy Joe would be her new boyfriend. He looked happy as his hands lightly touched the steering wheel, gently guiding the pickup truck to a quiet stop in front of her house.

"I'd like to invite you inside," said Bitsy, "but my dad would go berserk. It must be past one o'clock in the morning by now."

They laughed together. Then Billy Joe put on the emergency brake, hopped out of the cabin, and came around the other side to open the door for Bitsy. His hand was firm as he helped her to the sidewalk.

"I'll see you tomorrow night," said Bitsy.

"Of course," said Billy Joe.

Was it her imagination, or did the shy cowboy look as if he wanted to kiss her good night? She was fully awake now, with so many questions popping into her head. What's it like to live in a trailer? What's his family like? Can a small-town cowboy from East Texas find it in his heart to like a big-city girl from Brooklyn? Bitsy looked up into his sleepy blue eyes and knew she was in love. She wanted to see him tomorrow night. She wanted to be with him at the picnic. She wanted to do everything except say good night.

"Good night, Bitsy."

"Night."

And then he was gone. She stood outside listening until the sound of the truck faded into the stillness.

Chapter Fifteen

When her alarm rang at seven the next morning, Bitsy could barely drag herself out of bed. She surprised Marcia by graciously permitting Mrs. Mobley to drive the two young ladies to school.

"I thought you just loved to walk your legs off," said Marcia.

"I think my legs have fallen off," murmured Bitsy, and promptly fell asleep in the backseat, her schoolbooks sliding off her lap.

"I don't know about girls today," snapped Mrs. Mobley. "You're all a bunch of softies. Spoiled kids, every one of you. You don't have the energy, the get up and go, that we had."

Marcia turned around, shaking her head at

her sleeping friend. "Bitsy's get up and go got up and went."

Bitsy worked hard that day to stay awake and be attentive. During her American history class, she continually took notes, figuring the activity would help. At the end of that first hour, she looked down at her notebook and saw that she had scribbled Billy Joe Bridges all up and down the left-hand margin, the top of the page, and on the bottom line. The War of 1812 was surrounded by her love. In her science class, her math class, her English class, and her communications class, Bitsy continued to take notes. But Billy Joe was always there, guiding her hand, guiding her heart, whispering his good night while the instructors droned on and on. It seemed to Bitsy that the entire morning was a long-playing record and that the needle was stuck and the soloist, Billy Joe, was saying good night, over and over again. Bitsy was in a state of dreamy bliss, hearing his voice, seeing his face, over and over and over again.

At lunchtime, she met with Dave, Tony, and Specs. They sat at a corner table in the cafeteria, huddled together over hominy grits and black-eyed peas, discussing the lineup of songs, and singing harmonies under their breath. But their lunch was continually being interrupted by well-wishers. The student news program had announced that Bitsy and the Wing

Dings would be playing at the Chicken Coop. In fact, Elizabeth Ho had been broadcasting this hot news item all week long.

"Do you realize," observed Specs Glassberg, "that if everybody comes to the show tonight who came to this table today, there won't be any room for the tough customers? And then Bitsy won't get her story."

Bitsy's head was resting on her outstretched arms. When she heard her name, she sat up quickly, then looked around to see if she had been caught napping.

"As long as Billy Joe shows up, there'll be a story. I mean, as long as he brings the tape recorder. I mean. . . ."

"You mean," interrupted Dave, "you'd better take a nap. Because you don't know what you mean."

"Don't even go to work this afternoon," said Specs. "Get some sleep. We can pick you up."

"In Tony's car?" cried Bitsy nervously, suddenly realizing there was a transportation problem. "That car died last night. And all of us can't fit in Dave's two-seater. Maybe my dad can. . . ."

"Don't worry," said Dave. "My father is lending me his car. There'll be plenty of room."

"OK," said Bitsy. "Because the group has to stay together. We sing together. We drive together."

And then, at the opposite corner of the cafeteria, far across the long tables of noisy students, Bitsy's eye caught a group of cheerleaders parading out the door. A couple of denim-clad boys trailed behind them. Was Billy Joe one of them?

"Bitsy, are you with us?"

Tony gently prodded Bitsy into staying awake. But her mind kept drifting. She didn't care about flying soda cans at the Chicken Coop, or hoots or whistles. She only wanted Billy Joe to be there as part of her team, her special two-person team. She especially wanted him to be there at the end of the evening, at the end of this very long day.

"OK," announced Dave. "So I'm going to pick up Specs, Tony, and—you listening, Bitsy? —our beautiful female singer. . . ."

"Why are you picking me up last?" asked Bitsy.

"So you can get your beauty sleep," retorted Dave. "But be sharp and ready to wail at eight o'clock."

The group exchanged nervous smiles, then hurried off to their remaining classes. Bitsy could not resist a last look around for her cowboy.

The sun broke through large billowy clouds as Bitsy approached the Park 'N Pick parking lot that afternoon. A brightly colored van was pulling out, leaving the lot deserted except for Sue Ann Jones. Good, thought Bitsy. It's a slow day. Sue Ann won't mind covering for me. All Bitsy could think of was her warm, comfortable bed.

"Bitsy, honey, I've got a real favor to ask you," said Sue Ann as Bitsy approached.

"And I have a real favor to ask you."

"Well," said Sue Ann, "before you tell me your real favor, let me tell you mine. My old boyfriend is driving down from Dallas today, and I'd just love to see him. When you get yourself a boyfriend, I'll do the same for you. promise."

Bitsy took a deep breath, then made her way to the dressing room. All she could do was nod her head, which sent Sue Ann into squeals of delight. How could Bitsy stand in the way of love? How could she deny Sue Ann an afternoon of happiness? Besides, her friend's promise— "when you get yourself a boyfriend"—kept ringing in her ears. Bitsy looked at herself in the full-length mirror and said, "OK, this is no time for self-pity. Let's get out there and do some car-hopping!"

At six o'clock, the end of Bitsy's shift, Beau Chapparal drove up to Park 'N Pick with Betty Lou Bender.

"I'd like a chiliburger with everything on

it," said the Ice Queen. Bitsy leaned against the door of the white convertible.

"I'd like a ride home," said Bitsy. "Otherwise, I'll never get through the night."

Betty Lou was miffed, but Beau understood.

Bitsy took the rest of their order. Then, while they were eating, Bitsy quickly changed back into her sweater and jeans. Then she flopped into the backseat of the car.

"I really appreciate this," she said. "I'm absolutely dead."

Bitsy closed her eyes as Beau drove along the winding Red River Road.

"Beau," she said as he pulled into her driveway, "I want to thank you. That was really nice of you. And, Betty Lou, I hope you get to have your chiliburger."

"Oh, don't you worry about me, sweetie," she said, narrowing her eyes. "I'll have it with everything on it. And I mean *everything.*"

Bitsy groaned as she let herself out of the car and waved goodbye. But somehow, despite her tiredness and nervousness, she was able to realize that Beau had finally seen the light. He really had latched onto Betty Lou! Well, they were perfect for each other, Bitsy thought. Both shallow and superficial and in love with themselves. Still, Beau didn't seem to be mad at Bitsy, and that was a very tidy way for the whole thing to end. Now, if she and Billy Joe could just get something *started*. . . .

Three minutes later, Bitsy was stretched out in her bed, fully clothed, wondering if all these activities were really necessary. She was asleep before she could answer her own question.

Chapter Sixteen

It was the biggest white horse she'd ever seen
in her life. Certainly it was the biggest white
horse that had ever appeared on Flatbush Avenue, deep in the heart of Brooklyn. Bitsy whis-
tled softly. The horse approached and knelt
beside her. It had a rich tan leather saddle, and
Bitsy just floated onto it. She sat up straight as
the horse paraded along the avenue. But nobody took any notice of the horse or the rider.
The Roulettes were standing on a street corner,
harmonizing and clapping their hands. The entire club was out there, all of them wearing
their jackets. But none of them paid any attention to the cowgirl, who was wearing a white
Stetson hat, a short white jacket, and white

jeans. . . . Bitsy saw her mother on top of one of the roofs waving and waving and calling for Bitsy to come home.

Somebody was shouting Bitsy's name. Over and over and over again. Bitsy woke up. The room was in darkness, and for a moment, she didn't know where she was.

"Bitsy, are you in there?"

"Yeah," she shouted. "Be right there."

She rolled out of bed, literally, and landed on the floor, then fumbled along the walls, banging her knees against chairs. But finally her fingers found the light switch. And in the artificial light, she woke up. Seconds later, she was at the kitchen door, letting three worried musicians into the house.

"We tried to call you," said Specs, "but I guess you didn't hear the phone."

Bitsy was still feeling strange and disoriented, not adjusted to the time of night. Then the phone rang, further startling her. It was her father.

"What's going on there?" he shouted.

"I fell asleep," she mumbled. "But I'm OK now. The boys are here. We're about to leave."

"I'm sorry I'm late," he said. "But there was an emergency at the office. I hope I can get away to see you at this Chicken Coop place. But if I don't, good luck, and knock 'em dead!"

"Thanks, Dad." She hung up. The boys could see the disappointment on Bitsy's face.

"Man, we sure were worried about you," said Tony.

"Don't call me 'man,' " snapped Bitsy.

Tony turned to Dave and Specs. They all grinned. Bitsy was tough and feisty again, back in form. She ran into the bedroom. "Hey!" she shouted, as she changed into her all-white cowgirl outfit. "What if I forget the words?"

"Make 'em up," shouted back Specs.

"What if I forget the music?" she cried.

"You got three great back-up musicians behind you. Just snap your fingers and listen to us," shouted Tony.

"What if the customers throw things at us?" Bitsy asked, as she adjusted her white Stetson hat.

"Throw something back," said Dave.

When Bitsy entered the kitchen, she stretched her arms out so that the Wing Dings could admire her flashy costume.

Five minutes later, they were headed for Rowdy Row. Bitsy was no longer feeling quite so jittery about the lyrics or the music or the tough customers waiting for them at the Chicken Coop.

Chapter Seventeen

The guitar cases were spread out neatly in the luggage compartment of the Buick station wagon. Bitsy sat in the backseat, staring straight ahead at the open road. Next to her, Tony was humming nervously, tapping a harmonica with his fingers. In the front seat, Dave was steering with one hand and scratching his sandy-colored hair with the other. " 'Deep within mah heart lies a melodeee, a rose of old San Antone. . . .' " Dave knew all the old songs and was ready to sing each and every one at the drop of a Stetson hat. Next to Dave, a very serious Specs Glassberg was trying to assure Bitsy that performing in public was easy.

"It's like having a good rehearsal," he said.

"Hey," said Tony, "did we ever have a good rehearsal?"

Bitsy found herself feeling slightly sick. She turned around and looked back at the distant lights of Austin. Then she fell back in her seat and tried to concentrate on the passing traffic.

"Dave," she said, "is that a drugstore coming up on the right? I need some sugarless chewing gum to calm my frazzled nerves."

The station wagon swerved into the parking lot of an all-purpose grocery, pharmacy, and sandwich shop.

Bitsy tried to act casual as she asked Tony, "Did you see Billy Joe today?" But her beating heart was making a racket.

"He'll show up," Tony assured her.

She noticed Tony was getting increasingly nervous. "Don't worry," she told him. "Remember, we're performing a public service. The way those people act up when they dislike a group could cause a riot. Somebody could get hurt."

"Yeah," said Tony. "And I'm afraid it's going to be me."

She patted him on the head and got out of the car. The three young men just sat there, eyes straight ahead, waiting.

"Doesn't anybody want to accompany me?" asked Bitsy.

"OK," said Specs.

"Don't strain yourself," snapped Bitsy.

141

Specs sighed heavily and maneuvered his chubby frame out of the Buick. They walked in silence across the parking lot toward the glaring lights of the store.

"Did you see Billy Joe tonight?" asked Bitsy.

"As a matter of fact I did," said Specs. "He looked real strange, just sitting in his pickup truck, in front of the school, thinking hard. I never saw him so serious."

As they neared the brightly lit store, Bitsy tried to calm her nerves. But she wondered if the great love of her life was having second thoughts about the evening.

"Hey," said Specs, "maybe we'll be a big hit. Maybe they'll actually like us!"

"Yeah." Bitsy sneered. "And maybe Billy Joe will ask me to the class picnic. But don't hold your breath."

Five minutes later, Bitsy had her gum and was back in the car with the boys. Feeling considerably calmer, she held everyone's attention as she went over the lineup of songs. By the time they agreed on the order, Dave was making a sharp right turn into the huge parking lot, which was already filled to capacity. There was no big neon sign identifying the Chicken Coop, a heavy slab of cardboard with the name written on it in an almost childish scrawl was posted over the front door—a screen door half off its hinges. Bitsy and the Wing Dings lugged their guitar cases around the parked cars. When they approached the entrance, they met a long line of whistling, screaming young men. Some of them had dates. The girls were screaming as loudly as the boys.

"You think we should go through with this?" whispered Bitsy to Specs.

"Good music is good music," said Specs. "It's appreciated all over the world."

They passed the long line of youthful customers, most of whom were wearing jeans and T-shirts. Bitsy was at the head of the group, followed by Specs, Tony, and Dave. A big, fat bouncer blocked the front door. He had a beard that covered most of his face.

"Who are you?" he asked.

"Bitsy and the Wing Dings," announced Bitsy, adjusting her cowboy shirt and trying to look professional.

"Who and the what?" asked the man.

Dave came forward and identified everyone by name. The bouncer stepped aside, shaking his head and laughing.

"Y'all know how to make a person feel right at home," said Dave sarcastically.

The young musicians made their way along the side of the large, smoky room. To Bitsy, the bandstand seemed a hundred miles away. When she passed the first row of tables, she almost dropped her large guitar case. There, in the front row of tables, sat her father. He was with her communications teacher, Mr. Gonzales. She didn't have the faintest idea how they had met up. At the next table, Betty Lou Bender was sitting almost in the lap of Beau Chapparal.

"Good luck, Bitsy," said Beau, flashing his teeth and trying to hide his own nervousness.

Bitsy was about to ask him why he had a big leather bag under the table. Then she remembered—and shuddered. The tape recorder, the riot, the news story. She bit down on her lip and tried to relax. Where *was* Billy Joe anyway?

"Hiya, honey. Now don't be nervous."

It was her father, beaming down at her. Even in Austin, Texas, Mr. White looked like a New York City cop. In this blue-jean-infested community, he was probably the only man wearing flannel pants and black shoes. His white sports shirt hung over his belly and his belt.

"Hey, Bitsy," said Tony. "My whole family is here."

And, indeed, there were four tables of aunts and uncles and cousins, all of them focused on the pride of the Gomez family. Then Dave ran over and pointed to a tall, handsome lady sitting alone at a table way off on the side.

"That's my one and only mother," said Dave. "She's going to manage my professional career.

If you play your cards right, I'll introduce you to her."

Under more normal circumstances, Bitsy would have asked Dave to bring his mother to the ringside table with her father and Mr. Gonzales. But every part of her felt tense—her mouth, her eyes, her shoulders, her legs. Then she saw Specs standing by himself next to the chicken wire that separated the audience from the performers. It was supposed to protect the singers and musicians from flying objects thrown by the crowd, but it was no more than two feet high. Unless you're a midget, thought Bitsy, there's no kind of protection at all.

"Hey, Specs," shouted Bitsy, "come on over here."

"Where are your folks?" asked Bitsy.

"Back home in Rosenberg," said Specs. "I live with my grandmother. She said she was coming, but I don't think the Chicken Coop is exactly the place for a grandmother."

"Agreed," said Bitsy.

Way over by the rear exit door was a bench to which Bitsy and the group made their way. When they finally sat down and began tuning up, Bitsy felt calm enough to look around the dimly lit room.

And then she saw him. Billy Joe was pushing through the crowd to a single folding chair that seemed to be waiting for him directly in the center of the noisy room.

Bitsy waved several times, but he didn't see her. He was busy placing a small shoulder bag under the table between his legs. Bitsy knew that a tape recorder was inside the bag. She felt as if she were in a spy thriller.

And then, suddenly, the house lights went out. There was a momentary hush before the stage lights went on. The bouncer was in front of one of the microphones, looking out at the shouting, whistling audience. He did not hold up his hands to motion for silence. His presence was enough to quiet the house.

Bitsy leaned forward straining to see Billy Joe. But too many bodies were in the way. She could feel the tension rising as Dave, Specs, and Tony shuffled uncomfortably on their seats.

Let's get *on* with it, thought Bitsy.

"And now the Chicken Coop is proud to present"—the man paused and delicately took a scrap of paper out of his shirt pocket—"from Lubbock, Texas—Lasso!"

Five skinny, frightened young men wearing glittering silver shirts and white bandannas around their necks shuffled onto the stage. They tuned their guitars, checked the amplification, adjusted knobs, and mumbled to each other, trying to ignore the audience, which was getting noisier by the minute. The announcer had disappeared.

Bitsy quietly said a prayer for Lasso.

"Hey, Tony," said Dave, "y'all like the name Lasso? Pretty neat, huh?"

"How about just plain Rope?" suggested Tony. "Or Lariat?"

"How about the Wing Dings?" said Bitsy.

"How about keeping quiet?" said Specs. "We have to set an example. If musicians don't respect other musicians, how can we expect the audience to respect us?"

"He's right," said Bitsy. "Shut up, Dave."

Bitsy and the Wing Dings respected Lasso a good deal more than the audience did. The group from the small town of Lubbock was repeatedly advised to return to their homes. There were many imaginative suggestions as to the means of transportation. Halfway through the group's third song, objects began flying across the low-ceilinged room. The chicken wire did not help. The noise from the audience was now louder than the electronic music from the stage. The crowd was like a pack of wild animals. Certainly, thought Bitsy, this is no audience of school kids. Hyenas maybe, but humans? No way. She watched a barrage of beer cans. Then she watched the musicians make a quick exit. Finally, the fat man pointed his index finger straight at her and beckoned Bitsy and the Wing Dings forward.

Bitsy looked over at Billy Joe. Their eyes met—as if the vibrations between them were so strong their impulses overpowered the raucous room. Billy Joe stood up, smiled his cute smile, waved his beat-up cowboy hat, and let out a cowboy whoop.

Bitsy wanted to be next to him, to be carried by him out of the crowded room into his pickup truck. It didn't matter where they went. She would ask no questions. She just wanted to go. But her legs were carrying her up to the bandstand, past the tables, past her proud father, past her gently applauding school teacher, past a tight-lipped Beau Chapparal hunched over his bag. Bitsy thought Beau probably looked the same way on the football field, hunched over his center, calling out secret numbers.

"Hey, Dave," whispered Bitsy, "I can't breathe. What do I do?"

"Don't worry," said Dave easily. "Opening night nerves. Still got your sugarless gum?"

"I think I swallowed it," confessed Bitsy.

"Then take a few deep breaths," he said.

Specs got Tony and Dave and Bitsy together so they could tune their instruments.

"You kids ready?"

It was the fat man. Bitsy looked at each of her friends. They nodded solemnly back at her.

She tried to assume a nonchalant pose. "Ready whenever you are."

The fat man grunted and turned to the noisy crowd. "OK you guys, tonight we got the debut—like that word, debut?—of a bunch of high-school kids—"

"We're not high-school kids," hissed Dave. "We're professionals."

The fat man went right on talking. "—from San Jacinto High School way up north in Austin. So would you all give a real, down-home welcome to Bitsy and the Wing Dings."

The four tables of the Gomez family stood up and applauded loudly. Mr. White and Mr. Gonzales joined in. Bitsy was still nervous.

Then Tony began playing his bass guitar. Specs joined in with his rhythm guitar. Dave was right there, harmonizing on the fiddle, and Bitsy hummed the simple melody line of the Specs Glassberg composition, "Cotton Candy Cutey."

After the first thirty-two bars, Tony gave her a fresh downbeat and a nod, and Bitsy started to sing, " 'You taste so good to me, the way you should to me, you are the sweet thing that I love. . . .' " With each note, her voice grew stronger. The audience seemed to be attentive. The opening was a medium-tempo number, which allowed both the audience and the musicians to warm up together, to get accustomed to one another. By the second song, "Red River Rosey," the faster tempo had engaged the audience completely. Bitsy and the others were beginning to relax.

Suddenly there was a commotion. A sharp-faced young man with a crew cut, who turned out to be a security person for the Chicken Coop, had spotted Beau's tape recorder and tried to take it from him. Beau managed to wrestle the man to the floor, which gave Betty Lou enough time to get the recorder back in the bag. Then she made a fast getaway to the parking lot, while Beau was thrown out by the fat man. The mood was broken. The crowd was itching to let loose. Any excuse would do. It came with the next number, which was introduced by Tony.

"And now the band would like to play one of our latest songs: 'Where's My Tex-Mex Sweetheart?' "

Bitsy stood in front of the mike, listening to the guitar introduction by Dave.

Mr. Gonzales turned to Bitsy's father and whispered, "This is going to be tricky—a girl like Bitsy singing about her Latino boyfriend. Not the best choice of songs for a bunch like this."

His whispered words were prophetic. Bitsy had to duck a flying can of Dr Pepper, which was quickly followed by pretzels (salted) and peanuts (unsalted). More soda cans and beer cans joined the bombardment. Mr. White stood up and turned around to face the culprits.

"Knock it off," he commanded.

But this was no police bust, no disassembling of a street-corner crowd in Brooklyn. The retired police officer received a beer can squarely between his eyes. In the smoke and dim light, he could not make out his assailant. He temporarily sat down to nurse his forehead, cursing and fuming under his breath. He was fighting mad. So was Bitsy. She ordered the group to stop playing. Then she stepped forward and glared at the crowd. Like a professional, she waited until the noise level went down. The audience was a bit uncomfortable now, caught in the steady gaze of the lead singer.

"Would any of *you*," began Bitsy, "care to step up to the microphone and put yourself on the line?"

Silence. Specs, Tony, and Dave waited patiently, admiringly. She was doing what none of them dared to do—challenge the rowdy audience of the Chicken Coop. There were mumblings, rumblings, and coughs in the densely packed room.

Bitsy resumed singing "Tex-Mex Sweetheart."

A can of Lone Star Beer flew through the air and landed at her feet. Somebody shouted,

"Nobody likes a wisecracking girl," and a few brave men applauded in the darkness. Bitsy once again silenced her musicians. And once again she marched up to the microphone.

"Oh, yeah?" she snarled, in her best Brooklyn accent. "Why not?" She turned around to the group and called out the next number, "The Girl From Brooklyn." Now the audience was itching for trouble. They had been put down and silenced twice by this pretty little girl with the big voice. The opening eight bars were barely concluded when pandemonium broke loose. Bitsy's father and Mr. Gonzales managed to pick up some tables and use them as protection, while the Wing Dings and Bitsy made their exit. The last one out the door was Dave Mills, who had the last laugh, playing "The Eyes of Texas Are Upon You." And while Specs, Tony, and Bitsy joined in this traditional song—from the safety of the parking lot—Billy Joe Bridges quietly stood up. He held his old canvas bag loosely as he made his way through the room and out the front door. Outside, Bitsy saw him casually walking toward her, smiling shyly, and knew everything would be all right.

Chapter Eighteen

Bitsy looked into the beautiful blue eyes of Billy Joe. He had stopped some fifteen feet away from her and stood there, his mouth widening into a big grin. Bitsy felt his happiness, his confidence deep inside her. But she continued to stand where she was, and Billy Joe continued to stand where he was, like a smiling statue. Then a great crowd of well-wishers surrounded her. They were applauding and shouting her name, as well as Dave, Tony, and Specs's. It was like a football rally, right in the parking lot of the Chicken Coop. The Gomez family hugged and kissed Tony and then proceeded to hug and kiss the other Wing Dings. And ancient, gray-haired lady who couldn't have been more than five feet tall was squeezing Specs's arm.

"Hey, everybody," shouted Specs. "This is my grandma. Grandma, meet everybody."

The old lady smiled a beautiful smile.

Then Dave made an announcement. "Ladies and gentlemen, I want you to give a real down-home welcome to the greatest lady in the world—my mother—who started me on my brilliant career." The group applauded.

Then it was Mr. White's turn to blow a kiss to his beaming daughter. He didn't say anything; he just put his hands over his head like a boxer giving the victory sign. Then he turned to Dave's mother and said, "Our kids are pretty terrific, aren't they?" And she nodded emphatically.

Mr. Gonzales walked up to the station wagon, puffing on his pipe and looking very serious.

"Bitsy, I don't think there's anything more I can teach you about communications. I'm very proud of you."

And there was Marcia Mobley, in her designer jeans and an all-new permanent, beaming at her companion, Sue Ann Jones, who was hanging on the arm of a giant of a man.

"Bitsy," cried Sue Ann, "I thought you were sensational, honey. Now I want you to say hello to Max. Max plays football for the Dallas Cowboys. Max, say hello to my friend."

"You were good," said Max seriously. "Real good." •

But on the sidelines stood Billy Joe looking at Bitsy, not moving, not saying a word.

Bitsy wanted to go to him, but first she had to speak to Beau. And Betty Lou and Cesar Portillo and Elizabeth Ho.

Finally the crowd began to drift away. Bitsy found herself being lifted carefully off the ground by Billy Joe. He kissed her gently on the cheek before he set her back down.

"I've got some hot news," he whispered, "for next week's show." He picked up the canvas bag and slung it over his shoulder.

"Thanks," was all that Bitsy could say, her eyes shining with admiration and gratitude.

"Bitsy, I don't know if you have any plans for right now, but . . . umm . . . if you don't, I thought maybe . . . uh . . . you might like to go for a little canoe trip . . . just around Lake Austin."

Bitsy's head was filling up with questions: Where will you get a canoe at this late hour? and do you know how to handle a canoe? But her heart said yes, so she nodded her head and took his hand.

"You know, Bitsy, I just have to tell you that . . . well, I don't really care about being a rodeo star or a Texas Ranger. Those were just dreams."

"There's nothing wrong with dreams," said Bitsy, thinking about her own fantasies.

"What happened tonight," said Billy Joe, "was better than any dream. It was real. It was great." He swallowed hard.

She clung to his warm hand. "And so were you," she added quickly.

They were walking toward his pickup truck. Bitsy was so happy she glowed all over. She wanted to yell. She wanted to run. She wanted to grab Billy Joe and hug him hard. But instead, she just walked quietly beside him, smiling broadly, waiting for him to speak again.

"I bet we'll do the 'Dirty Laundry' story, too, someday. We'll find a way. We'll be a team!" said Billy Joe excitedly.

Bitsy just beamed some more. Then she gasped. She remembered she hadn't said good night to the Wing Dings or congratulated them or anything.

The clear accent of a New York cop cut through the stillness of the night. "Kind of late to be taking out my daughter, isn't it?"

Bitsy turned around, expecting to see the stern, reprimanding face of her father. Instead, she saw her father as if for the first time—with a sad look in his pale green eyes. It was the look he'd had for her mother, when she had told him she was leaving.

"I guess my little girl's not so little anymore," he said.

Billy Joe reached for his hand and shook it.

Bitsy giggled. She figured Billy Joe probably milked a cow with the same motion.

"My name's Billy Joe Bridges," he said, his voice rising as if he was asking a question and needed confirmation about his name. "I'm a good friend of your daughter besides being a fellow student and a fellow worker at KALL." He sounded like he was applying for a job.

"I guess that makes you quite a fellow," said Mr. White.

"Oh, *Dad*," said Bitsy, shaking her head.

"Young man," said Mr. White, "I want you to drive carefully. And please don't get my daughter home too late."

"Sir," began Billy Joe, "I'm an excellent driver. I have great respect for your daughter. And I don't smoke or drink."

"OK, kid," said Mr. White. "I guess you check out."

For a second, Bitsy thought her dad was going to frisk Billy Joe. But he simply kissed his daughter on the forehead and walked away.

"Be right back, Billy Joe," said Bitsy.

She ran to the Buick station wagon and planted great big kisses on the cheeks of her three favorite musicians. They were beaming. Dave let out a real Texas shout. "Eeeyahooo! Let's hear it for Brooklyn, New York!"

Specs blushed a deep red and cleared his throat several times. "Thank you, Bitsy," he said, in his most mature voice.

But Bitsy wasn't truly happy until the Chicken Coop was behind her. Then she sat contentedly next to her blue-eyed cowboy with the gentle smile. She looked around to see if she could see into his eyes or read his thoughts. He looked quite serious.

"Bitsy, I've been asking a few questions myself, and I hear you're not going to the school picnic with Beau. I wondered if you might like to go with me—that is, if you don't have any other plans."

For once, Bitsy had no questions of her own in her head. She took a deep breath. "I'd love to go with you to the school picnic," she said.

There were times, she thought, when life really could be so simple.

Chapter Nineteen

Bitsy sat back in the canoe and let her hand caress the cool water of the lake. Overhead were more stars than she had ever seen before. Billy Joe pointed out the Big Dipper and the Milky Way and the North Star.

"So that's the Milky Way," exclaimed Bitsy. "I thought it was just a candy bar."

Billy Joe put the paddle in the water and guided the canoe away from the boathouse, out toward the dark lagoon. The shoreline was still in sight as he let the canoe drift along past the large willow trees. Their melancholy branches dipped into the still water. For a long time, the only sound was the paddle pushing the canoe through a watery dream world.

Billy Joe began talking about what growing up on a farm with horses and pigs and chickens and cows was like.

"Sounds great," said Bitsy.

"Nothing great about it. A farm's like a factory, except there're no days off. The nearest school was miles away. So was the nearest town. On Saturdays we used to go there and watch haircuts for entertainment."

"Watch haircuts?" asked Bitsy, thinking he was kidding.

"Yeah," said Billy Joe. "That was one of the big events. That and smelling bread. There was a bakery on Main Street. We used to hang around, smelling all those fresh rolls and cakes. And bread."

Bitsy looked around at the long, tangled vines growing down into the watery channel. Billy Joe had paddled them to a narrow part of the lagoon, where great boulders on either side shut out the real world.

"No cows in Brooklyn," said Bitsy. "Maybe a few horses. The only chickens were all wrapped up—you know, in supermarkets. Lots of pigs, though. Some of my best friends were pigs." She giggled. And Billy Joe threw his head back and laughed.

"Not much fresh bread, either," said Bitsy. "Just packaged stuff. The worst. I never knew what a fresh tomato tasted like until we got to

Austin." She leaned back in the canoe and studied the stars, wondering if Billy Joe wanted to kiss her. Then she wondered if a girl should kiss a boy or wait for him to kiss her. They do things one way in Brooklyn, she thought, but this is Texas. Whatever *that* means.

Billy Joe pulled the paddle out of the water. The canoe continued to drift. And then without warning, he leaned forward, the canoe hardly stirring, and kissed Bitsy. It was a warm, gentle kiss. His lips lingered on her lips. His breath smelled cool, sweet, inviting. She returned the kiss.

Afterward Bitsy pulled back, inhaling deeply. "Wow." She sighed. "Can I ask you one or two questions about that kiss?"

Billy Joe stared at her, not knowing whether to laugh or get angry.

Suddenly they heard the sound of strumming guitars. Somewhere near the lagoon someone was playing a love song.

"How perfect," whispered Bitsy.

The canoe drifted around a bend. Before Billy Joe and Bitsy could see where they were, two enormous lights were switched on, illuminating them and blinding them at the same time. As they turned their heads away, blinking and rubbing their eyes, the music stopped.

"Some clowns are carrying on over there," snapped Billy Joe. "And I'm getting mad."

Now the night air was filled with the sound of rich voices, male voices singing "The Eyes of Texas Are Upon You," thumping on guitars like they were a marching band. Billy Joe began paddling furiously toward the big lights.

"Oh, no!" shouted Bitsy. "It's the Wing Dings!"

Dave obediently switched down the car lights. "Surprise!" he cried. "Just wanted to catch the lovebirds."

"Very funny," shouted back Bitsy.

"Hey, Bitsy," yelled Tony. "Beau Chapparal has a message for you. Says he wants to take you to the picnic after all."

Billy Joe put the paddle in the water, stopping the drift of the canoe. Then he began to push away from shore, away from the serenading young men.

"You tell Beau Chapparal," he shouted, "that Bitsy is spoken for. Oh, yeah, and tell him that the Question-Mark Kid is getting all her answers from Billy Joe Bridges."

Tony, Specs, and Dave began clapping and yelling. Then on a cue from Dave, they resumed singing and playing "The Eyes of Texas."

"Billy Joe," said Bitsy, "I am certainly not getting all my answers from you or from anybody."

He was paddling swiftly now through the

lagoon, back out toward the middle of Lake Austin.

"And furthermore," she continued, "what do you mean by 'spoken for'?"

"Well," said Billy Joe. "That's sort of like . . . lavaliered."

"Lavaliered?" repeated Bitsy. "What's 'lavaliered'? Are you trying to get serious?"

She opened her mouth to ask another question, but Billy Joe silenced her by putting his finger on her lips and saying "Shhh." She stared into his beautiful blue eyes, her heart beating wildly. For the moment, all her questions were being answered.

Read these great new *Sweet Dreams* romances, on sale soon:

( ) **#29 NEVER LOVE A COWBOY by Jesse DuKore** (On sale December 15, 1982 • 23101-4 • $1.95)
Bitsy is thrilled when she moves from crowded New York City to colorful Austin, Texas, and even more thrilled when she sees handsome Billy Joe riding his horse to school. But even when Bitsy's new school radio program grabs everyone else's attention, Billy Joe's eye remains on gorgeous Betty Lou. Can a city girl like Bitsy ever win the heart of a Texas cowboy like Billy Joe?

( ) **#30 LITTLE WHITE LIES by Lois T. Fisher** (On sale December 15, 1982 • 23102-2 • $1.95)
Everyone says Nina has a good imagination—a gift for telling stories. In fact, it's one of her stories that attracts Scott to her. He's one of the Daltonites, the most sophisticated clique in the school. The Daltonites don't welcome outsiders, but Nina finds it so easy to impress them with a little exaggeration here, a white lie there. But her lies finally start to catch up with her, and Nina's afraid of losing Scott forever.

( ) **#31 TOO CLOSE FOR COMFORT by Debra Spector** (On sale January 15, 1983 • 23189-8 • $1.95)
For years Drea and Derek have been best friends. They've always loved each other, but when Derek asks Drea for a date, their feelings grow stronger, until finally they're *in love*. Then things start going sour for Drea. Is it because

Derek's becoming so possessive? Or because Sam Henessy's getting interested in her? Should Drea break up with Derek? And if they do, can they ever be friends again?

( ) **#32 DAYDREAMER by Janet Quin-Harkin (On sale January 15, 1983 • 23190-1 • $1.95)**
All too often, Lisa finds herself escaping into daydreams—dreams of fame, friends and boyfriends galore, Hollywood, her parents, and falling in love. But when her fantasy bubble bursts, she has to open her eyes to the fact that, in real life, things don't always work out the way they do in dreams.

( ) **THE LOVE BOOK by Deidre Laiken & Alan Schneider (On sale January 15, 1983 • 23288-6 • $1.95)**
If people could recognize true love at first glance, life (and love) would be a lot less complicated. But love is not always what it appears to be. The more you know about love, the more successful you'll be at finding and keeping it—and understanding love is what this, the first nonfiction *Sweet Dreams* book, is all about.

Buy these books at your local bookstore or use this handy coupon for ordering:

Bantam Books, Inc., Dept. SD11, 414 East Golf Road, Des Plaines, Ill. 60016

Please send me the books I have checked above. I am enclosing $_____ (please add $1.25 to cover postage and handling. Send check or money order—no cash or C.O.D.'s please).

Mr/Ms_____

Address_____

City/State_____ Zip _____

SD11—12/82

Please allow four to six weeks for delivery. This offer expires 6/83.

You'll fall in love with all the Sweet Dream romances. Reading these stories, you'll be reminded of yourself or of someone you know. There's Jennie, the *California Girl*, who becomes an outsider when her family moves to Texas. And Cindy, the *Little Sister*, who's afraid that Christine, the oldest in the family, will steal her new boyfriend. Don't miss any of the Sweet Dreams romances.

☐	22542	**LOVE SONG #19** Anne park	$1.95
☐	22682	**THE POPULARITY SUMMER #20** Rosemary Vernon	$1.95
☐	22607	**ALL'S FAIR IN LOVE #21** Jeanne Andrews	$1.95
☐	22683	**SECRET IDENTITY #22** Joanna Campbell	$1.95
☐	22840	**FALLING IN LOVE AGAIN #23** Barbara Conklin	$1.95
☐	22957	**THE TROUBLE WITH CHARLIE #24** Jaye Ellen	$1.95
☐	22543	**HER SECRET SELF #25** Rhondi Villot	$1.95
☐	22692	**IT MUST BE MAGIC #26** Marian Woodruff	$1.95
☐	22681	**TOO YOUNG FOR LOVE #27** Gailanne Maravel	$1.95
☐	23053	**TRUSTING HEARTS #28** Jocelyn Saal	$1.95
☐	23101	**NEVER LOVE A COWBOY #29** Jesse Dukore	$1.95
☐	23102	**LITTLE WHITE LIES** Lois I. Fisher	$1.95

Buy them at your local bookstore or use this handy coupon for ordering:

Bantam Books, Inc., Dept. SD, 414 East Golf Road, Des Plaines, Ill. 60016

Please send me the books I have checked above. I am enclosing $_____
(please add $1.25 to cover postage and handling). Send check or money order—
no cash or C.O.D.'s please.

Mr/Mrs/Miss _____

Address _____

City _____ State/Zip _____

SD—1/83

Please allow four to six weeks for delivery. This offer expires 7/83.